Will the new girl run for queen of the Fall Festival?

"And our last nominee," Mrs. Gallagher announced, "is Gwenyth Darby!"

I smiled, more out of nervousness than anything else, and glanced down at my shoes. I couldn't bear to look at the other students. Especially Tony. There was a respectable amount of applause, but I could hear someone behind me say, "Who's Gwenyth Darby?"

"So . . . what are you going to do?" my friend Doyle asked me.

I'd been asking myself that question for twelve straight hours. A beauty pageant at my new school? Me? Still, I couldn't stop thinking about what my twin brother said the night before—about taking on a challenge and standing up to the reigning establishment. That *was* me.

The gym was almost empty now, but Bree Hampton—fellow nominee—and her clones were huddled together, whispering and glancing at me. A chorus of snickering welled up from the group, and Bree lifted a cold gaze in my direction.

Suddenly it was as if a switch had been thrown, and my old cool, determined self—the real me— came out of her hiding place.

"I'm going to do it," I said to Doyle, turning to meet his stunned stare. "I'm going to accept the nomination for queen of the Fall Festival."

Super Edition

Three Princes

LYNN MASON

BANTAM BOOKS
NEW YORK · TORONTO · LONDON · SYDNEY · AUCKLAND

RL: 6, AGES 012 AND UP

THREE PRINCES
A Bantam Book / December 2000

Cover photography by Michael Segal.

Copyright © 2000 by 17th Street Productions,
an Alloy Online, Inc. company, and Jennifer Ziegler.
Cover art copyright © 2000 by 17th Street Productions,
an Alloy Online, Inc. company.

Produced by 17th Street Productions,
an Alloy Online, Inc. company.
33 West 17th Street
New York, NY 10011.

ISBN: 0-553-49329-9

Visit us on the Web! www.randomhouse.com/teens

Published simultaneously in the United States and Canada

Bantam Books is an imprint of Random House Children's Books, a
division of Random House, Inc. BANTAM BOOKS and the rooster
colophon are registered trademarks of Random House, Inc. Bantam Books,
1540 Broadway, New York, New York 10036.

PRINTED IN THE UNITED STATES OF AMERICA

OPM   0 9 8 7 6 5 4 3 2 1

Thanks to Joe, Louise, and Max McDermott, George Sanger, Randy Henderson, and Jason Ford for all of your help. Thanks also to Renee, for sleeping.

Dedicated to my three princes:
Carl Ziegler, Owen Ziegler, and Jim Ford

One

Cameron

I'D HAD SUCH great plans for my senior year in high school. I wouldn't work as many hours at the garage. I'd hang out with friends more. And most of all, I'd finally get up the nerve to ask out Ashleigh Witherspoon—the girl I'd had a crush on for eight years. But so far, nothing had gone right.

On the second day of school my mom injured her back and had to go to a special hospital in Houston (the docs said she'd make a full recovery). My dad had closed up his auto-mechanics shop and had gone with her, which meant I had to stay with my aunt Lenore and my cousin Blaine, who lived on the other side of town (Kingstown, Texas) in a huge house. To make things worse, Aunt Lenore seemed to think my main purpose in living with her was to do her bidding.

Such as fixing her car (which needed more help

than I could give it) and driving her around. Aunt Lenore came from a very wealthy family, but she'd fallen for my dad's brother, Bert, who'd been a carpenter, and married him twenty years ago. She owned a lot of land in Kingstown, including the country club. My parents' house was on the proverbial wrong side of the tracks, mostly because Mom and Dad were very content to raise their family (meaning me) on their own hard work. I had to admit, I respected that.

I slammed down the hood of her BMW and went back inside the house. Aunt Lenore was pacing in front of the dining-room table as if she were in a hospital waiting room.

"How's the car?" she asked as soon as she saw me.

"She needs a new belt, Aunt Lenore." I placed the flashlight back in the tool drawer. "There's no way you can drive it today."

"A new belt? Oh, my." Her painted-on eyebrows knitted together in worry. "Will it take long to fix that?"

"Not normally," I answered, "but with Dad's shop closed, I'll have to call Barney and have him send me a new belt. Once it arrives, it should only take a day or two to put it on and recharge the battery."

"Oh, dear." Aunt Lenore shook her head, her big, red hairdo moving as one unit. "Well, I suppose I'll need you to drop me off at work on your way to school. Let me make a call, and then I'll meet you outside."

As soon as she disappeared, I let out an exasperated

grunt. How much longer would this go on?

I walked to the kitchen sink to wash off the engine grime and caught sight of a small framed photo of Uncle Bert and Aunt Lenore on the window ledge. "Hey, Uncle Bert," I said.

Uncle Bert had been like a best buddy to me, and I missed him something awful since he died from a stroke five years ago. That was one reason why I couldn't complain about doing so much for Aunt Lenore. She wasn't cruel—just clueless. Uncle Bert had always taken care of the house and cars and even served as the handyman at the country club. She'd had no one to do that stuff for a while now and had to rely on Blaine, who never did anything.

"Cameron, dear! I'm ready!" Aunt Lenore called.

"Coming!" I replied, drying my hands on a nearby towel.

We left the house and walked down the long, circular driveway. Aunt Lenore's typically fast trot slowed a little as we approached my orange 1978 Volkswagen Beetle. When I opened the passenger door, she reached down and dusted off the vinyl seat before climbing inside.

"I suppose I'll be needing a way to work this week," she said as I pulled onto the road.

"I can give you a ride, Aunt Lenore," I offered.

"Oh, good! Thank you, Cameron." She sat back in her seat and started dusting off her shoulders. "And since I'll be needing a ride home, would you mind coming by the club after school and waiting for me?"

I groaned inwardly. Just the thought of that

high-society place made me uneasy. "I guess so."

"And as long as you're there, I'll need you to do a few repairs. The Fall Festival queen pageant is going to be held in the ballroom, and as chairperson, I have a million things to do to get ready. Everything has to be perfect. Why, just the other day Mrs. Pear told me . . ."

My mind wandered off. Aunt Lenore always seemed to forget that I had no real interest in all this.

". . . and it's such a shame that Ashleigh Witherspoon isn't eligible," Aunt Lenore went on.

"What?" I asked. The sound of Ashleigh's name made me tune back in.

"That's right," she said. "Since her father is the mayor, they won't let her compete. It really is too bad. She would make the perfect queen."

She really would, I thought, letting my mind drift off again. Ashleigh was just plain perfect. I should know, having been in love with her so long. She was nice, smart, easygoing, and beautiful. On any given moment I could automatically conjure up her face: her wide smile, cocoa-colored eyes, and oh-so-touchable-looking blond hair.

I pulled the car up to the front door of the Kingstown Country Club and stopped, my mind still whirling with thoughts of Ashleigh.

"Cameron? Cameron!" Suddenly Ashleigh's face melted away, replaced by Aunt Lenore's pinched features.

"I'm sorry," I said, blinking hard. "Did you say something?"

Aunt Lenore stepped out of the Volkswagen, dusted herself off, and poked her head back in. "I said, I do hope you can get to work on my car right away."

"Don't worry, Aunt Lenore," I said. "I'll fix it as soon as humanly possible."

Marissa

"Waffles or French toast?" My mother waved a spatula at me as I entered the kitchen.

"Just cereal and coffee, Mom. I'm running late." I slid into the chair opposite my dad—or at least I assumed it was my dad behind the City-Metro section of the *Houston Chronicle*—and began filling a bowl with Special K.

"What do you know? Not even a mention of Fall Fest in their 'Around the Town' column," came a mumbling from behind the paper. "What? We're not slick enough for them?"

Yep. It was my dad, Ernesto Valdez, back there.

"It's probably because we're two hundred miles away from their city limits," I pointed out. "That's not exactly 'around the town.'"

Mom set a steaming mug in front of me and sighed. "You know, you really shouldn't drink coffee. That's probably why you're so glum all the time. If you'd just let me make you a nice omelette."

"Mom, no. Really."

Food. That's Mom's answer to everything. If I'm sick, I need food. If I'm tired, I need food. And if I seem more pissed off than usual, I obviously haven't eaten enough vegetables. How we all managed to stay thin was beyond me.

Dad lowered his paper and stared at me, his dark brown eyes crinkling up like tissue paper. "It's not an omelette that this girl needs," he said.

"Finally!" I exclaimed. "Someone on my side."

"What she needs is to get out more. Socialize with friends," he added.

Then again, I could have spoken too soon.

"That's true," Mom said, nodding. She set down her plate of waffles and sat down at the table. "Why don't you ever go out anymore, sweetie? You never invite anyone over or talk on the phone."

Oh no! Not this *speech again!* "Mom!" I whined. "Do you realize how you sound? Most parents are upset that their kids slack off all the time, hanging out and talking on the phone. You actually have a mature daughter who cares about more important stuff. You should feel lucky."

"Lucky?" Dad folded up the paper and set it on the empty chair seat to his left. "I want to know why you're so grown up all of a sudden. Why are you suddenly too good for everyone? When a nice guy calls and asks you out, you turn him down. Why?"

"Dad!" I shut my eyes and pressed my fingers against my temples. "You aren't going to start talking about Will Benson again, are you?"

"Yes, I am. That boy is polite and respectable. And you don't get to be the star pitcher on your school baseball team by slacking off. Maybe you should go out for a sport too. At least you could put on school colors once in a while instead of dressing like someone died."

I gripped my coffee mug and tried to ignore my dad. I really didn't want to argue and get him all riled up since it was bad for his health. Ever since Dad had a heart attack four months ago and was forced to retire early from the accounting firm, he'd been on my back way too much. He still had a few accounts around town, but basically his main line of work had become scrutinizing my life and trying to turn me into some all-American Barbie doll.

Last year, when I started going out with Will Benson, Dad couldn't have been happier. But I was miserable. Will treated me like dirt, I never had any fun, and I realized all my social-climbing "friends" were just looking for ways to stab me in the back. Then when Dad got sick, everything changed. I decided to stop wasting energy on all that phony stuff. So I dumped Will, stopped hanging out with the wanna-be popular girls, focused on my art more, and traded in my trendy clothes for more individual ensembles. I figured, if school was just a long, depressing game, then I should dress accordingly.

A loud engine noise suddenly drowned out my dad, who was still rambling about my antisocial behavior.

"What the—" Dad jumped up and peeked outside the kitchen window. "It's that kid again! That loony from across the street!"

Speaking of antisocial. Fry Darby must have just left for school.

7

Two months ago we got new neighbors, a family from New York City. One of them was a guy my age. His name was Brian, but everyone at school called him "Fryin'" or "Fry" for short—basically because he was an obvious burnout who rode a motorcycle. Half the town was terrified of him, but mainly he was just annoying. As my luck would have it, he ended up in my advanced-art class, but I hoped at any moment he'd realize he didn't belong there and drop out. The other was his sister, Gwenyth, who didn't seem to drive dad to hysterics.

"Darn hoodlum!" Dad exclaimed. "I know that crackpot is up to no good. I see him at night, drinking beer on their roof! And I'll bet anything he's behind all those mailbox vandalizings."

I smiled secretly as Dad ranted. I didn't like Fry either, but at least he'd managed to take the focus of my dad's anger off me.

"Well, I'm off," I announced, heading for the door.

Dad shook his head. "I think I should drive you today. I don't want you walking to school when that guy is out there."

"Dad!" I whined. "I'll be fine! It's not like he can kidnap me on a motorcycle. Besides, he's probably halfway to school by now."

He scowled at me while he considered this. Eventually he nodded. "All right," he grumbled. "But promise me you'll be careful."

"I will, Dad," I said, quickly stepping out the front door before he could change his mind.

"And don't accept rides or talk to anyone," he called out after me.

"Okay!" I shouted while I practically ran down the sidewalk.

Girl, you have really got to get a life, I thought bitterly. *You know things are bad when you can't wait to get to school.*

Gwenyth

"And I already got the evening gown this past summer when my mom and I went to California," Bree Hampton said. "We got this incredible strapless dress. It's perfect for the pageant."

I watched as Bree paused long enough to look at each of us, as if checking to make sure we were still holding on to each word. Then she did her trademark wiggle thing—sticking her pointy nose up in the air and shaking her head back and forth until all her hair settled behind her shoulders. A wiggle or two later and she continued.

"Of course once we came home, I had to look everywhere for the right shoes. I swear, there's no decent shopping around here."

"Ugh, I know," Linda Loftin agreed.

Bree barely paused to blink at Linda. "But I finally found some when we went to visit my brother in Austin. Now I can focus on my talent piece. It's going to be killer. I'm going to . . ."

My mind shut down. My ears failed. My eyes

blurred from being forced to stare at Bree for the past twenty minutes. Jeez! How long was she planning on talking about this dumb contest? You'd think nothing else was going on around here.

Then again, probably nothing else was.

It had been less than three months since my folks moved us from New York City to this scab on the face of the earth. My mom and dad were sick of doing commercials and got hired to run the theater program at South Texas College in Farhills. You should have heard them when they broke the news to us. They sounded like two kids at a birthday party. Needless to say, my twin brother, Brian, and I were less than thrilled. Mom and Dad kept telling us how great it would be for us, how we wouldn't have to mess with traffic or crowds or pollution anymore. But two days after we moved here, I was so bored, I would have gladly taken that stuff back.

My brother and I had gone to a school for the performing arts when we lived in New York. He studied art and sculpture, while I had a dance concentration. When we started going to Kingstown High, I checked to see if there were any ballet classes and was told they only had something called a "dance squad." Meaning: Girls dress up in little cowgirl outfits and do high-kick routines during halftime at the football games. Not exactly what I'd call "dance," but I thought I'd at least meet some girls with the same interests as mine. So, I started hanging out with the senior girls on the squad, who also hung around with the cheerleaders, who also—it turned out—were the snootiest girls in the school. Oh, a couple of them, like Linda Loftin and Sherry Wynn, were actually pretty nice. But they were so under the total brainwashing direction of Bree, the school's head cheerleader, they couldn't form a thought for themselves. Whatever Bree said went, and no one had the guts to cross her.

"Don't you think so, Gwen?" I glanced up and saw Bree smiling at me—the kind of smile where the mouth turns upward, but the eyes seem to be sneering. I guessed she was put out that I wasn't hanging on her every word anymore.

"Huh?" I asked. "What did you say?"

She sighed slowly. "I said, 'Don't you think it's better if I choose country music for my routine?' The judges probably aren't into 'N Sync, right?"

I wanted to say: *How the heck should I know?* Instead I nodded and said, "Oh, right," because I was also too gutless to stand up to Bree. Being new, it just seemed better to go along with the status quo rather than become an outcast right from the start.

The bell rang, and the entire student center jump-started with activity. Our group mumbled their obligatory "see ya's" and splintered off in different directions. I sighed in relief. Advisory wasn't exactly the high point of my life, but at least I didn't have to listen to Bree anymore.

I heaved my knapsack onto my shoulder and shut my eyes, trying to pretend the voices and footsteps I heard were echoing off the walls of the Perry Reese School for the Performing Arts. My old friends were there. The teachers let us call them by their first names. The cafeteria served sushi. . . . As soon as the image was complete, I took a step forward and ran right into something that was big and solid and smelled like Calvin Klein cologne.

I opened my eyes and found myself staring at a Goo-Goo Dolls concert T-shirt, the design oddly distorted by the wearer's bulging chest muscles.

"You okay?" T-shirt wearer asked.

I looked up into the face of Tony Etheridge. It wouldn't be exaggerating to say that Tony was the best-looking guy in the school—I noticed that on day one. He was also the guy Bree had stamped her name on. They weren't a couple yet, but for weeks she'd been saying it was only a matter of time before they hooked up. He was probably as much of a pea brain as the other guys I'd met (more so if he had a thing for Bree), but it still made me swallow to see him smiling down at me, his head haloed by the yellow fluorescent lights.

"Um, yeah," I replied. "Sorry. Just wasn't looking where I was going."

"I noticed," he said, laughing slightly. There was something about his eyes. . . . Oh, they were as green and gorgeous as I remembered. But something about the way they looked at me was making my skin feel hot and clammy.

"Sorry," I said again, forcing myself to look away before my tongue dropped out of my mouth. I hadn't been this close to a sexy guy in months and was out of practice at keeping it cool. In New York,

12

I'd never had that problem. How did I get so dorky so fast? "I'm just used to walking fast, being from New York and all."

"Right," he said, nodding.

"I guess I don't really need to, though. You guys are really slow. I mean, slow as in *walking* slow, not mentally slow. You guys aren't stupid. Well, probably some of you are, but not all of you." Suddenly I couldn't stop talking. The clammy feeling was spreading by the second.

The left corner of Tony's mouth lifted in a sort of half smirk, and he took a step toward me. Again his musky scent wafted over me, and I wouldn't have been surprised to feel my skin slide off my body.

"There's one thing you need to learn if you're going to stay here," he murmured.

"Oh? What?" I practically whispered.

"It's 'y'all,' not 'you guys.'" Tony's wide grin re-extended itself, and then he turned and started walking down the hallway—slowly.

Dear Cameron,

Just wanted to let you know that the treatment continues to go well and your mother is doing fine. She enjoyed your last letter very much.

I know that before we left you were upset about having to move in with your aunt Lenore. We realize that you are capable of taking care of yourself. Your mother, however, would be making herself sick with worry every day if we had left you at home alone. That's just how mothers are. And she doesn't need that kind of stress now while she's in

13

recovery. Besides, your aunt Lenore is a good woman, and it's better to be with family during these times.

I hope you and Blaine are having fun hanging out together. Your mother says she misses you and sends her love.

Take care,

Dad

P.S. We are very grateful to Lenore for doing us this favor. Try to help her out now and then, okay?

Two

Marissa

I WALKED INTO school and was immediately bombarded with noise as everyone made their way to advisory. Luckily I'd been assigned Coach Mackinatt. The first three weeks of school I would ask him if I could go work on my advanced-art project, and he'd always let me. Now I just went straight to the art room without even checking in with him.

The screeches and laughter and other annoying sounds muffled to near silence when I entered Ms. Crowley's room. I sighed in relief. This was the only room in the whole school where I felt I belonged.

As I headed to my usual workstation, I heard a pounding sound behind me. *Oh no,* I thought. *Please don't let it be him again.*

I glanced over my shoulder and saw Fry Darby smacking around a large piece of clay. Immediately my mood turned sour again. For the past few days

Fry had been coming here during advisory to work on his sculpture of . . . something. I couldn't tell what. I had hoped it was just for a couple of mornings. But now it was becoming clear that, like me, he intended to do this every day. It bugged me to no end that I'd have to share the peace and quiet with some thug who probably didn't know the first thing about serious art.

I picked my project off the holding shelf, sat down, and took out my pencils—totally ignoring Fry. Pulling back my hair with a clip, I bent over the drawing, trying to focus. My sketch of a vase of sunflowers was coming along slowly. Something didn't seem right. Maybe if I just . . .

Wham! Wham! Fry pounded his clay behind me, making me jump.

I shut my eyes and took a deep breath. No wonder I couldn't sketch well. It was a miracle I could work at all. I turned around and glowered at him, hoping he'd get a clue.

Fry didn't even see me. It was amazing he could see anything with his long, gnarly hair in his face. I continued glaring at him, hoping the heat from my stare would eventually penetrate his ripped Johnny Bravo T-shirt and make him look up.

"Don't worry. I'm done," he muttered without raising his head.

"What?" I asked.

"I said, I'm done priming the clay," he repeated. "I won't be making any more noise for a while."

"Good," I replied, trying to keep an edge to my

voice. It bugged me that he wouldn't even glance up at my death stare. Although considering I couldn't even see his eyes, maybe he had and I didn't know it.

"Just the people I wanted to see," Ms. Crowley announced, breezing through the doorway. A vision of yellow. Her long, blond braid and long dress were the color of wheat. In fact, the dress might have been *made* out of wheat for all I knew. Ms. Crowley was the town hippie as well as the town artist. Her sense of fashion was fodder for gossip almost as much as Fry's.

She strode over to her desk and picked up a small square of pink paper. "I got a message this morning from Mrs. Gallagher at the country club. She needs someone to paint a backdrop for the Fall Festival queen pageant, and I volunteered the two of you."

Fry and I glanced at each other. *Me* work with *him?* A cold feeling of dread spilled through my veins. There was no way. I'd either end up dead or accused of attempting to murder him.

"I can't," I protested. "I don't have time."

"Yeah. Me either," Fry echoed.

"You two will have plenty of time," Ms. Crowley said in her evenly measured tone. "You can meet here before and after school, and I'll let you use the class hour. I'll give you both extra credit. . . . "

The chilly sensation running through me seemed to harden into ice. "But what about my project?" I whined like a baby. "I can't stop working on it—it's really coming along." That was a bold-faced lie, but who cared?

17

"Can't you find some other guys?" Fry asked.

She shook her head. "All my other students are already making floats or working the face-painting booth to help raise money for a new airbrush. I know you and Marissa think you're too advanced for this sort of thing, but you need to do it."

I let my head flop forward into my hands. This was just too much. Not only did I have to paint a stupid picture for a beauty contest, but I had to do it with Fry Darby! I looked at Fry, who was staring at the ceiling, shaking his shaggy head. At least he didn't look any happier about it than I was.

"Please," Ms. Crowley said gently. "I really need your help."

Fry exhaled loudly. Then he glanced up at Ms. Crowley and nodded slightly. "I'll do it. I guess," he said. "Now, may I please be excused to wash up?" He held up his clay-smeared hands.

"Of course, Brian. Thank you." Ms. Crowley's tranquil, peace-and-love pose returned as she turned toward me. "And what about you, Marissa?"

I stood and walked over to her desk. "You know I'd do anything for you, Ms. C. Even this. But do I have to work with *that?*" I gestured toward the door.

Ms. Crowley's smile disappeared, and for the first time in two years I could tell she was mad at me.

"I can't believe you said that, Marissa," she scolded.

"Hey, I don't *hate* him or anything," I tried to explain. "I just don't think we could work together. We're too . . . different."

Ms. Crowley sat quietly for a moment, still condemning me with her eyes. Then she looked down at her hands. "Sleep on it, Marissa," she said. "If by tomorrow morning you still don't think you can do this, I'll figure something else out."

I sighed in relief. She understood!

"But I want you to think hard about this," she added, that trademark peaceful grin returning to her features. "Really long and hard."

Cameron

I practically ran to my second-period English class. Not because I found Mrs. Langtree's teaching of *Beowulf* particularly exciting, but because this was the only chance all day that I'd get to see Ashleigh.

As soon as I crossed the threshold into Mrs. Langtree's room, I eagerly glanced at her. To my surprise, she was smiling at me. Before I lost my nerve, I headed her way.

"Hey," I said.

"Hey," she repeated. "What's up?"

A simple enough question, but it totally stumped me. What was up? My pulse rate? My blood pressure? *Think, Cam!* "Uh . . . do you have a pen I could borrow?" *Auugh! Did I say that?*

Ashleigh's head bobbed up and down, her glossy blond hair rippling around her face. "Yeah. I'm sure I have one in my bag."

She leaned over and unzipped her brown leather

satchel, rummaging among its contents. I took the opportunity to briefly shut my eyes and get a grip. I couldn't believe how complete a loser I was. It took guys years to approach Ashleigh, and when I finally got there, I asked for a measly pen? Never mind how lame and unoriginal it sounded. Never mind that I had five ballpoints in my own knapsack. I owed it to myself to do better.

I sat down at the empty desk next to her and leaned forward. I figured I should at least take this opportunity to make small talk—and use my entire brain this time. "So . . . I heard you aren't allowed to run for Fall Fest queen. Is that true?"

"Yeah. But I don't care," Ashleigh said matter-of-factly, still bent over her satchel. "I'm already sick of Fall Fest, and it hasn't even started. It's all my dad can talk about right now."

I laughed. "Tell me about it. My aunt's so worked up about running the pageant, you'd think it was a vital international-peace conference."

"Hey, at least you don't have to be in the thing." She glanced up and rolled her eyes. "My dad's actually making me ride on the float with him and the grand marshal."

"Who's that going to be?" I asked, trying to extend the conversation as much as I could. I couldn't remember ever having talked with her this long.

"Dad hasn't decided yet," Ashleigh replied, reaching way down into her bag. "It'll be tough. According to festival rules, he has to select a senior ~y who personifies 'the true spirit of Kingstown.'"

"Someone boring?" I asked.

Ashleigh's head snapped back up. She stared at me with an openmouthed smile before bursting out laughing. "I think that's the first joke I've ever heard out of you." She cocked her head and squinted at me, as if studying a biology specimen. "I mean, you're usually so quiet in school. Except for that time in physical science when Mr. McCorkle got you talking about combustion engines."

I suddenly became self-conscious. I know she meant to be nice, but her statement only reminded me how out of my league I was trying to talk to her. I felt like some dweeby little kid who knocked on her door, selling cookies.

Ashleigh must have noticed how miserable I'd become because her own face fell slightly. She leaned forward and placed her hand on my forearm. "Hey, um . . . I've been wondering. How's your mother?"

I blinked at her. My mother? How did she know about my mother? "Uh . . . fine. She's better. Thanks."

"Good." She gave my arm a slight squeeze. My skin felt warm and prickly where she'd touched it, and I fought the urge to put my own hand on the spot.

"All right, find your seats, everybody!" Mrs. Langtree's voice suddenly cut through the chatter. It startled me so much, I jumped to a standing position.

"Here you go," Ashleigh whispered, pressing a pen into my hand.

"Thanks," I managed to whisper back. Then I slowly ambled toward my desk, cradling the pen between my palms as if it were some rare and valuable artifact.

Wow. Just this morning Ashleigh had been a remote vision. Now we'd actually had a conversation. She'd even touched me!

Maybe my luck was changing. Maybe my senior year would turn out to be great after all.

Gwenyth

"I hate this place," my twin brother, Brian, announced as he barged into my room.

"Then don't come in here," I suggested, barely pausing to glance up from my homework.

"No." He sat down on my bed and flopped backward, his ratty Converse sneakers still planted on the floor. "I mean I hate this town and all the phonies who live here," he explained to the ceiling. "Man, I wish we were back in New York!"

"Yeah," I replied, my voice thick with self-pity.

"Everyone's so nerdy here," he went on. "It's amazing the calendars aren't still on the last century. All they care about is pickup trucks and football."

I'd been thinking these exact same things for weeks now, but it somehow made me irritated to hear him say it. I guess because it just reminded me how miserable I was.

Brian sat up and faced me, and his upper lip contorted into a fierce scowl. "Have you heard everyone going on about this Fall Fest thing?

What's up with that? You'd think Elvis himself was going to rise from the dead to give a concert." He snorted slightly, smirking at his own joke.

"Yeah, well," I muttered noncommittally. Knowing my brother, he wanted me to get all worked up with him. If I didn't, he'd do one of two things. He'd either try harder to rile me or get frustrated and leave me alone. I was praying for the latter.

"I'm so tired of everyone acting like we're from Mars," he went on. "They think just because we come from New York, three things must be true about us." He held up his left fist and began counting off fingers. "One: We're good friends with David Letterman. Two: We're card-carrying members of the Mob. Three: We must know their cousin so-and-so who moved there a couple of years ago. Don't they realize that millions of people live in New York City?"

At this point Brian leaped to his feet and began pacing around my room, waving his arms in disgust. My hopes sank. Obviously he wouldn't be getting frustrated and leaving anytime soon.

"They think I'm a freak just because I don't dress like a Garth Brooks clone. They figure I do drugs because my hair isn't in some U.S. Army square cut. They call me 'Fry' and joke about the sawed-off Uzi in my backpack." He quit stomping around, pausing in front of my vanity mirror to frown at his reflection. "Face it, Gwen," he grumbled. "We're in hell."

That did it. I couldn't take any more. Not because

I didn't agree with what he was saying, but because I did. It doesn't make sense, I know. If you've never had a brother, you wouldn't understand.

"Hey! Don't say 'we'!" I shouted, slamming my textbook shut and spinning around in my chair. "At least I'm out there trying to make friends. But you . . . you act as if you don't care what people think!"

Looking him over, I could almost see why everyone made those stupid assumptions about him. Brian had always verged on the skater look, but since we'd moved here, he started totally slacking off in the looks department. He wore his seediest clothes, let his hair practically go to dreads, and didn't bother to shave regularly. If I didn't know how sweet and sensitive (and good-looking) he really was, I'd be scared of him too.

"What's going on, Bri?" I asked, lowering my voice. "How come you won't give it a shot here?"

"Since when are you such a Kingstown fan?" Now it was his turn to yell.

"Hey, I'm not crazy about this place either. All I'm saying is that you've changed. Why have you gone so grunge? It's like you *want* people to think you're some burnout."

"Maybe I do." Brian slouched back against my vanity, rattling my bottles of perfume. "I mean, you can't convince people they're wrong about that stuff. Not really. So I let them think they're right about me. Now I sort of like that they leave me alone all the time."

I folded my arms across my chest and frowned at him. "But if you're all jazzed about this strategy,

24

how come you're in here complaining?"

Brian grinned slowly. Obviously I'd seen a major flaw in his cover. "I don't know," he said. "My art teacher, the one cool person I know, is making me paint backdrop scenery for this beauty pageant they're having."

"For Fall Fest queen?" I asked.

He raised his eyebrows. "You've heard of it, huh? Man, I can just imagine. They'll probably want me to do a little hearts-and-flowers design. Someone shoot me." He closed his eyes and shuddered dramatically.

"Big deal. You had to do stuff you didn't like at the arts school," I pointed out.

"I know." He shrugged. "But there's this girl they're making me work with. She's sort of . . ." He paused for a second, shaking his head. "I don't know. I just hate it when they force us to buddy up."

"Why? Is she some slacker who'll make you do all the work?"

"No. She's good, actually. She just hates my guts." He sighed. "You know how it is. There's no one here we can actually talk to, not like we talked to our friends in New York. No one worth the trouble."

Tony Etheridge's face suddenly flashed through my mind. I thought of the way he joked with me that morning. *He* seemed worth getting to know. Brian had to be wrong. This place couldn't be all bad, could it?

"Looks like we just have each other," Brian said, reaching over and grabbing my nose affectionately.

"Now you've totally bummed me out," I honked.

Brian laughed and released his grip. "Anyway," he said, heading toward the door, "thanks for letting me spaz out. I'll get out of here now."

I stared at the doorway for a couple of moments after he left. I felt bad for Brian. In New York, I was sort of jealous of him. He was known around school as this artistic genius. The teachers loved him, and everyone wanted to be his friend. Now all that had been taken away. No wonder he'd given up.

I wondered if I'd be better off if I ditched the "in" crowd and became a loner like him. I wouldn't have any friends, but at least I wouldn't have to go all phony.

No, I thought, resting my head on my hand. *He might deal with stuff by avoiding it altogether. But not me.*

I'll make this move work out one way or another—no matter what it takes.

KINGSTOWN HIGH HERALD
"QUOTATION REMARKS" COLUMN

Question: "What do you think is the best part of Fall Festival?"

LINDA LOFTIN, SENIOR: "The elementary-school floats. They are so cute!"

BRIAN DARBY, JUNIOR: "The what?"

BREE HAMPTON, SENIOR: "Everything. Fall Festival has to be the high point of every year!"

BLAINE GALLAGHER, SENIOR: "The parade."

MARISSA VALDEZ, JUNIOR: "Nothing, really. I mean, this is going to be something like my fifteenth Fall Fest. After a while it gets old."

Three

Marissa

I HEADED TOWARD Kingstown High, which loomed like a brown brick pimple at the top of the hill, only a few blocks away from my house.

All last night I tossed and turned, trying to decide what I should do about Ms. Crowley's offer. On the one hand, it was nice of her to give me an out. As it was, I hated working with partners. I'd much rather do things myself. And the thought of doing the project with Fry Darby, of all people, gave me a feeling of heavy dread—as if a giant hand were pulling me down by the intestines.

Then again, she'd hinted pretty blatantly that I'd be letting her down if I backed out. I knew she probably thought I was being unfair, but I wished she'd get real. It didn't take a Mensa member to see that the guy had what people would call "issues." And considering how much I already hated school, having to buddy up with that guy for several days could send me over the edge.

Still, Ms. Crowley had done so much for me these past two years. In fact, she was probably the only person I really liked in the entire school. The question was, did I want to avoid Fry more than I wanted to risk disappointing Ms. Crowley?

A noisy pickup truck roared past, and I veered to the far side of the sidewalk and tripped over something. I stood and dusted myself off, glancing around to see if anyone had watched me take a spill. Then I checked to see what I'd stumbled on: a wooden post with THE THURSTONS hand lettered on it. The mailbox vandals had struck again.

I knelt down and examined the damage. Bits of blue-painted wood were strewn across the front lawn, and the flattened mailbox lay on a nearby hedge.

What jerks, I thought, picking up the plank of wood with the name on it and tossing it onto the rubble on the grass. I wasn't exactly crazy about this town either. But at least I didn't go around wrecking it.

"Hey, Marissa!" someone yelled. I spun around and saw Will Benson hanging out the driver's-side window of his Bronco, which had slowed to a crawl. "Let me give you a lift."

Oh, man! Just what I needed. "No thanks," I said, staring straight ahead.

"Aw, come on!" he called out. "What? You afraid I'll kidnap you and take you across the border?"

I rolled my eyes at the irony of it all. How I wished I could tape-record his words and play them back for my father. Will Benson, who could do no wrong, joking about harming his only daughter. I ignored the comment and kept walking.

"Really. You don't have to worry. I left my ropes and chains at home. Course, you might actually like that stuff," he went on. I could hear his lackey, Lenny Pipkin, snickering from the dark interior of the car. God, what losers!

"Seriously, though. I've been meaning to tell you—I really like the new bad-girl look. Reminds me of Faith from *Buffy the Vampire Slayer*. Only sexier."

"Get lost!" I snapped.

"Uh-oh," Lenny gasped in false alarm. "Witch woman is getting angry."

"Yeah. We better go before she turns us into frogs," Will added.

Their creepy laughter grew fainter and fainter as they drove away.

I stood there, fuming. Deep down, I knew those guys' comments weren't even worth the sound waves they created, but it still irked me.

A sudden feeling of déjà vu came over me. *Is that what Ms. Crowley's trying to tell me?* I wondered. *That I'm judging Fry the same way those guys are judging me?*

I took a deep breath and started walking even faster toward school. Finally I'd made up my mind. I would help out Ms. Crowley and do the stupid project with no fuss. I'd show her how mature I could be.

Besides, artists had to suffer for their craft anyway. Right?

Gwenyth

I shuddered as the cafeteria lady plunked a large biscuit onto my tray with a loud thud. It seemed to me that a biscuit shouldn't make a noise like that, but what could I do? She passed my plate along to another woman in a hair net—this one in charge of the vegetables.

"Oh God," I mumbled, wincing as she spooned a far too generous serving of some mustard yellow, lumpy substance onto one of the tray slots. "Please let that be creamed corn."

"I'm fairly certain it is," said a voice next to me. "Although I'm not positive it's actually creamed corn from *this* century."

I turned and faced the guy ahead of me in line. I recognized him instantly. Slight build, freckles, and thick red hair that exploded wildly from his scalp. He was in my calculus class first period. I'd forgotten his name, but I remembered that he was incredibly smart.

He must have noticed my partial recollection of who he was because he gave a sideways grin and said, "I'm Doyle Jackowski. I'm in your—"

"Math class," I finished for him. "Yeah, I know. I'm Gwen Darby."

"I know." He gave another lopsided smile.

I glanced at my tray, which was getting a giant dollop of some new lumpy substance. "Mashed potatoes?" I guessed aloud.

"Correct," Doyle answered. "Hey, be glad. At

30

least this time they peeled the potatoes first before they made it. Ah . . . now here we go on to the finishing touch. The meat dish."

I followed his gaze back to the serving line, where yet another cafeteria worker had commandeered my tray. She slapped something brown and floppy onto my plate, then covered it with several spoonfuls of dull gray gravy. I could feel my stomach start to retreat downward, hiding somewhere behind my appendix.

"Ugh," I exclaimed, wrinkling up my nose. "That'll teach me to leave my lunch at home."

Doyle nodded. "All it takes usually is one time. Then you never forget it again."

"Is that what happened to you today?"

"No," he replied. "Some overfed bully on the bus thought it would be comical to toss my lunch bag out the window into a cow pasture."

My mouth dropped open. "That's awful!"

Doyle shrugged matter-of-factly. "Those are the realities of high school. Well." He picked up his tray and pivoted toward the noisy lunchroom. "Good luck eating."

"Same to you," I replied.

As I wended my way around the crowded tables toward my usual spot, I could see the back of Bree's head bobbing around and her perfectly manicured hands gesturing wildly. She was already revved up to full speed.

"I mean, really." Her voice grew louder as I approached the table. "You'd think he shops at

31

Goodwill. And she probably shops at some place called Tramps Are Us."

There she goes, I thought wearily. *Busy socking it to some poor slobs.*

As I came up behind Bree, the other girls' eyes widened, making them look fearful and uneasy. But why?

Then I listened more closely to Bree.

"Think about it. Her hair is so short, she looks like a four-year-old boy. And his hair is longer than mine! Maybe that's the way all the burnouts dress in New York, but you've got to wonder. Do they, like, trade clothes at home?"

A cold realization seeped through me, paralyzing me in place. Bree had been talking about me and Brian! How long had *that* been going on?

"Gwen!" Linda Loftin called out, a little too cheerily. "We were wondering where you were!"

Bree twisted around to face me. "What's wrong?" she asked, looking me up and down. "Too many drugs last night?" She snickered and turned back to face the others, making sure they'd appreciated her joke.

My fingers tightened on the cafeteria tray as I pictured her face smeared with creamed corn and gravy.

"Come sit next to me, Gwen!" Linda said, patting a stool beside her.

My mind froze up briefly and then restarted. I couldn't believe Linda was acting like nothing was going on. Was she hard of hearing or in total denial? Did she actually expect me to just park myself next to her and start eating, pretend everything was normal?

Then it occurred to me. That was exactly what she expected. Because that was exactly what she and the other girls would do. They'd rather stomach the snide remarks than stand up to Bree.

I fixed my gaze on the back of Bree's big, permed hairdo, letting my anger loose. "I can't, Linda," I said, still glowering at Bree. "Someone's fat ego is taking up all the room."

Bree turned and narrowed her eyes at me. "Oh? Then where *will* you sit?" She lifted her chin and smiled smugly.

I quickly glanced around the cafeteria. Okay, where could I sit? I hadn't exactly thought that far ahead.

Suddenly I spotted Doyle sitting two tables over with a few other guys. They were watching me and Bree. Holding my head high, I walked over and sat in one of the empty chairs next to them and began casually spooning mashed potatoes into my mouth.

Bree's high-pitched cackle reverberated through the air. "Great. Go ahead and sit with the losers," she called out. "Just remember, that's where you belong." Then she turned back to the others, lowering her voice to gossip level again.

Linda flashed me a sympathetic look and then stared down at her food. I knew she wouldn't be rushing to my defense—none of them would. I wondered what I'd done or said to be outed from The Group by Bree. Maybe I hadn't been hanging on her every word enough. Whatever. I didn't care anymore. Getting away from that group of phonies, even though it meant social suicide, still gave me a small sense of relief. At least I didn't have to pretend anymore.

I suddenly noticed Doyle and the other guys at the table staring at me quizzically. "Uh . . . sorry," I said self-consciously. "Is it all right if I sit here?"

"Sure," Doyle replied. "Guys, this is Gwen Darby. As you probably know." The rest of the gang nodded, a couple of them flushing pink. I wondered if a girl had ever sat with them before.

"Gwen, allow me to introduce you to our gang," Doyle continued. He turned to his immediate left and proceeded to go around the table, gesturing to each one. "This is Bennett, Haskell, Rom, Oscar, and the twins, Larry and Terry."

I smiled and nodded at each guy, a couple of whom I also recognized from my classes. It was the science-genius crowd, the ones Bree and the rest always referred to as the Geek Gang.

"Please don't mind me," I said, cutting a bite of mystery meat. "Go back to whatever you were talking about."

They eyed each other nervously. Finally Bennett mumbled, "So . . . as I was saying, online multiplayer mode is where the real action is."

"That's bull." Terry shook his head vigorously. "Multiplayer is boring. All you get are a bunch of 'newbies' as cannon fodder since they're too dumb to figure out the game."

"Except for Final Fantasy or the Ultima realm," Oscar jumped in. "Those people know what they're doing."

Haskell gave a dramatic yawn. "Oh yeah. It's

really suspenseful when you have a bunch of role-playing ninnies saying things like 'forsooth.'"

"Guys, guys," Doyle said, holding up both hands. "Enough with the gaming debate. We're going to make our guest feel out of place."

"Don't worry about it," I said, shrugging. "Actually, I was about to say I prefer Zelda myself."

Cameron

I dipped a spoon into the simmering concoction and carefully slurped it into my mouth. All it needed was another dash of cayenne pepper. I stirred in the ingredients and turned down the heat.

I'd decided to make Cam's Famous Tongue-Scarring Chili since Aunt Lenore was working late at the club and Blaine, as usual, was playing golf. After reading Dad's letter, I realized how unfair it was for me to be feeling sorry for myself. Dad had enough stress trying to help Mom. Mom sure didn't need the distraction. And it was really cool of Aunt Lenore to take me in. Besides, she really could use some help now that Uncle Bert was gone.

I whistled as I arranged the corn on the cob on top of a big, fancy platter and placed it on the table. The tune was a love song I'd heard on an episode of *Dawson's Creek*. It had been ringing through my head ever since I'd talked to Ash earlier that morning. Just spending that short bit of time with her made everything feel dreamlike, as if I were in a TV show of my own.

The front door opened, and footsteps echoed in the foyer. "Cameron, honey? Are you here?" Aunt Lenore's voice sang out.

"In the kitchen!" I called back.

A moment later Aunt Lenore and my cousin Blaine stepped through the swinging doors.

"Oh, my!" Aunt Lenore exclaimed, glancing around the room. "What is that I smell?"

"Chili," I answered. "Enough for all of us."

"Oh, my!" she said again, placing both of her hands over her heart. "Aren't I lucky? My dear nephew is making me dinner. And just this afternoon my darling son offered to stay and play an extra round of golf at the club so he could give me a ride home!"

Ooh, yeah. Real big of him, I thought. "Go ahead and sit down. It's ready." I gestured toward the dining room.

"Thank you, Cameron. I'll do that." Aunt Lenore spun around on her high heels and trotted away.

Blaine flashed me a disgusted look. "What? You think you're going to win favors this way? You think you're gonna get something by doing this?"

"Just dinner," I said. I turned off the burner under the chili, slipped on two pot holders, and hoisted the heavy, cast-iron saucepan.

"Hey, doughboy," Blaine taunted, poking me in the ribs. "Where's your apron?"

I clenched my teeth, forcing myself to stay calm. "Blaine, unless you want burning-hot chili all over your khakis, you better get your hands off me."

Blaine jumped back, and I resumed my way to the dining room.

I wasn't going to let him get to me now. Not today—the day I'd finally had a real moment with Ashleigh.

We ate in silence for a while. I could tell Aunt Lenore thought it was too spicy, but she politely picked at it. And it amazed me how she ate corn on the cob—by cutting the kernels off with a knife and eating them with a fork. Blaine, on the other hand, wolfed down his food like a rottweiler.

"So . . . ," Aunt Lenore said, dabbing the sides of her mouth with a cloth napkin. "I'm going to be needing some assistance from you boys these next several days. Could you two please come by the club and do a few chores after school?"

"Sure," I replied.

Blaine mumbled "kiss up" while pretending to cough into his hand.

"And you, Blaine, dear?" Aunt Lenore asked.

"Can't, Mom. These next few days are going to be real tough. I've got all this extra homework and stuff. I'm usually too tired after golfing, so I have to get up early and do it. You don't want me to start getting bad grades when school's just started, right?" Blaine shot his mother a big-eyed, innocent expression—as innocent as one can look with a kernel of corn stuck to his chin.

"I suppose you're right. Don't worry about it, honey. I'm sure Cameron and I can manage." She reached over and patted Blaine on his hand.

"Sorry I can't help you there, cuz," Blaine said with a smug smile. "You know how it is."

I couldn't believe Blaine managed to get out of every single favor Aunt Lenore asked of him. I was glad I wouldn't have to work with him, but if I stayed late at the club every day, I wouldn't have time for anything else. That meant I wouldn't have time to go out with Ashleigh.

A hot, panicky feeling spread through me, as if the chili I'd eaten had just caught fire. "Um . . . Aunt Lenore?" I said. "If I work real hard these next few days, could I have a night off so I can . . . go out on a date?"

Blaine cackled loudly. "A date? With who?"

I squeezed my hands together, trying to prevent them from choking Blaine. "I'd rather not say," I mumbled.

"Blaine, that was rude," Aunt Lenore chided. "A gentleman always respects another's privacy." She turned and smiled at me. "Cameron, you are free to do as you like one of these evenings. Just as long as you finish clearing the boxes out of the banquet hall."

I breathed a sigh of relief. "No problem, Aunt Lenore. Thanks."

"Oh, *and* set up the PA system," she added. "We really need to test that. And maybe you should at least pick up the risers at the rental place. But you don't need to set them up right away. Of course, then again . . ."

As I morosely stirred the remainder of my chili

around the bottom of my bowl, an image of Ashleigh's face danced in front of me. She was smiling, just like she had earlier that day. Only as Aunt Lenore rambled on, the image seemed to get farther and farther away. . . .

The City of Kingstown is offering a
$100 Reward
for information leading to
the capture of any person(s) responsible
for the recent string of mailbox vandalism.
Please contact the police with any helpful details.

Four

Gwenyth

THEY WERE STARING at me. All of them. I'd just sat down and unwrapped my turkey sandwich, trying to act like everything was normal. But the rest of them eyed me as if I'd just landed in my seat by way of parachute.

"You know," Doyle finally said, "I think you already made your point. You don't *have* to sit with us again."

"I know I don't have to. I want to. That is"—I looked around into each of their faces—"unless you don't want me here?" A jittery feeling came over me. Suddenly I feared another social group was casting me aside.

Doyle held up both of his hands. "No. It's not that. We like you being here. We just didn't want you to feel obligated."

"You don't have to do it for us," Haskell said,

the large reflection of his eyes in his bifocals blinking at me reassuringly.

"Yeah," Bennett chimed in. "We would understand if you're worried about your reputation."

"My reputation?" I asked. "Do I have a reputation?"

"Oh no!" Bennett blushed so deeply, his freckles disappeared. "I just meant that . . . when you . . . it's sort of like . . ."

"He means that if you're seen with us, you could be labeled one of us," Larry finished for him.

"One of you?" I repeated stupidly. All I'd wanted was to sit down with people I knew (which wasn't many), totally ignore Bree, and eat my turkey on rye. Now I had seven pairs of eyes (eight if you counted the mirror image in Haskell's glasses) staring at me as if I were about to jump off the roof of the gymnasium. Even with a full curriculum, I was suddenly finding lunch to be my hardest hour of the day.

"Yes. One of us. The geeks," Doyle explained. "Otherwise known as dorks, nerds, dweebs, eggheads, or—my own personal favorite—goobers. There seems to be some theory going around that if you sit with a geek, you start to smell like a geek, and then, before you know it, you are classified as belonging to the genus and species *Geekus maximus* yourself."

I'd heard this stuff before. Bree was constantly handing out social demerits to people for either dressing the wrong way, riding the bus, attempting a subpar hairstyle, or being seen with someone she considered less than worthy.

"Who cares?" I said with a wave of my hand. "It's a free country. I'll sit where I want."

The seven of them glanced at one another, as if they were silently communicating with invisible antennae.

After a brief moment Doyle turned to me and smiled. "All right, then. Cool. But don't say we didn't warn you."

I slowly resumed ingesting my sandwich and tried to look as blasé as possible in case Bree was watching. I'd purposefully sat with my back to my former table of "friends." But occasionally I could hear Bree's trademark titter—like an asthmatic chicken—and I knew she was laughing about me. I had to admit, I was sort of curious to know why I'd been banished. Perhaps Bree had always been making fun of me behind my back. But then why let me into her little clique in the first place?

"Hey, Gwen." A deep, smooth voice jarred me out of my thoughts.

I turned and saw Tony Etheridge standing behind me. It felt like my pickle had crawled back up my throat and wedged itself on top of my voice box. "Hey," I croaked. *What the heck is he doing here? How does he know my name?*

"You've got Mr. Peabody for government, right?" he asked. His forehead crinkled up, making his sea green eyes seem larger and droopier than usual.

"Yeah," I said, nodding casually while inside my mind a miniature search-and-rescue operation was being launched. *How does he know I have Peabody? How does he know anything about me?*

"Great." He hunkered down beside me, his eyes level with mine. I could feel his breath on my arm. I could smell the fabric freshener on his shirt. I could count the individual lashes surrounding his eyes. It was dizzying to have him so near.

Tony balanced an open spiral on his bent knee. "I forgot to write down the reading assignment yesterday, and I have his class next period," he explained. "Could you tell me what it is?"

"No problem," I said. I opened my backpack and started digging through it, wondering whether Tony needed all this for real or if it was some sort of ploy to talk to me. Usually I had pretty accurate radar about such things, but ever since I'd moved to Kingstown, I seemed to have lost my knack.

"So . . . ," Tony began, filling the awkward silence, "I was looking for you at your friends' table. Why are you sitting here?"

"Why not?" Doyle snapped.

His answer startled me. I'd been so busy swooning over Tony, I'd almost forgotten he and the others were there.

"She can sit where she wants. So why not here?" Doyle went on.

"Whoa," Tony replied, standing up slowly. "Look, I only meant—"

"Oh, we know what you meant, don't we, guys?" Doyle asked. But the rest of the gang sat frozen in place with their eyes as wide as compact discs.

Tony's face clouded over. I couldn't tell if he was angry, embarrassed, or totally shocked.

43

"Take this," I said, ripping the assignment page out of my spiral and pressing it into Tony's hands.

Tony stared at the paper with a befuddled expression. I wondered if Doyle's outburst had made him completely forget his intended mission.

"Go ahead," I told him. "I had that class last hour, so I don't need it anymore."

Tony looked at me, glanced over at Doyle, then looked at me again. "Thanks," he mumbled, and slowly walked off.

"Why'd you do that?" I demanded of Doyle as soon as Tony was out of earshot.

"Yeah, Doyle," Terry said. "You could have gotten us all killed!"

"I was just trying to protect you," Doyle said, looking right at me.

"Protect me?" I echoed.

"Great," Rom mumbled. "Protect her but sacrifice our lives."

"Yes, protect you," Doyle said again. He leaned across the table toward me and lowered his voice. "Look, you're new, so there are things you probably don't know about Tony and the other football thugs. Those guys have only two purposes in life: tormenting the smarter kids and trying to get as many girls as possible."

"What are you saying?" I asked.

"I'm saying he's bad news. Just ask any of these guys." Doyle waved his thumb toward the rest of the gang. They nodded solemnly. "Think about it, Gwen. He comes over with some lame excuse about

44

homework? Please! The guy was coming on to you."

My face must have brightened at the thought because Doyle shook his head reproachfully.

"Don't do it, Gwen," he said. "Sure, he's a pretty boy, but he knows it. Jocks go out with girls, treat them terribly, then dump them. He came over here looking for a fresh victim to ask out."

"Or beat up." Haskell moaned.

A sick feeling slowly crept over me. Doyle was right. Maybe it wasn't shock that had made Tony clam up after Doyle's outburst. Maybe it was guilt.

Little by little, it seemed like everything potentially good about this town was turning out evil.

Marissa

Okay. So I did it. I told Ms. Crowley as soon as I got to school yesterday that I'd do her dumb project with Fry. Good for me, right? Wrong. She was thrilled, of course. Then she told me we should start working on it as soon as possible—like after school today.

Bad for me.

I could feel my stomach overflow with anxiety as the art room loomed into view. It made me so angry that the one place I enjoyed in this stupid school was now a major source of stress. Still, I'd given my word. It was too late to weasel out now.

I sucked in my breath and opened the door. The first thing I saw was Fry, standing in the middle of the room with a piece of slate gray charcoal paper in his right hand. His left hand rubbed his stubbly chin, and he stared at the drawing hard, as if it were one of those 3-D images that make you go cross-eyed.

"Nice work," he said without taking his eyes off it.

Suddenly it felt like icicles were stabbing through me. That wasn't just any sketch he was looking at—it was *my* sketch!

"Hey! Give me that! That's mine!" I yelled like some six-year-old kid.

Fry didn't even blink. "The scale is great, but your shading is off."

"Who do you think you are?" I snarled. "Give me that now before I kick you!" I reached over and snatched the sketch out of his hands, wrinkling it slightly.

"Hey, I was only trying to help. Some thanks I get." He had the gall to sound offended.

For a moment I just glowered at Fry, wishing I could rub him out with a big chunk of Artgum. Then my mouth reactivated. *"Thanks?"* My voice practically sizzled. "You expect me to thank you?"

Fry held up his hands and shrugged. "At Reese we always critiqued each other's pieces. You don't have to take the advice, but it helps usually. I mean, if you're thinking about living the life, you better get used to critics."

I was returning my drawing to the work-in-progress shelf when his words froze me in place. Suddenly I forgot my anger. I turned and gaped at him. "You . . . you went to *Reese?* Perry Reese School for the Performing Arts?"

"Yeah." He slunk into a chair, propping his grungy Converse sneakers on the worktable. "You've heard of it?"

Heard of it? The guy had been living my dream! Reese School was one of the premiere secondary art schools in the country. In fact, I'd halfway convinced my dad to let me try to get in there for my junior and senior years. But that was before his heart attack. Now with him living off retirement, I knew better than to push it.

All this time I'd assumed Fry was in art just to be bohemian. I never thought he really knew what he was doing.

"So aren't we supposed to be planning the backdrop thing?" he asked, folding his hands behind his messy hair. "Because if not, let me know. I'll motor home."

His cynical tone snapped me out of "duh" mode. *Get over it,* I told myself. *Just because he went to Reese doesn't mean he's not a jerk.*

"Let's just come up with an idea today," I said, taking a seat across from him, upwind from the Converses. "We still have plenty of time to do the real work."

"Cool. So what are your ideas?"

I frowned. "What are *your* ideas?"

"Okay." He took down his feet and sat forward in his chair. "I was thinking maybe we could do something colorful and abstract, sort of cubist looking."

"For a *beauty* contest?" I asked, halfway laughing.

"Okay, then." Fry sat back in his chair abruptly. "Let's hear your great ideas."

I shrugged. "How about an Old West theme or autumn leaves?"

Fry wrinkled his nose. "Seems a little obvious. Don't you think?"

"Well, they're better than your idea!"

"You never even considered my idea," he snapped. "You dismissed it without even seeing a sketch."

I crossed my arms and glared at him. I knew he was right, but I silently waited for a good retort to come.

"I know what you did." His face went blank, and his voice became low and monotonous. "I know you begged Crowley to get out of doing this."

I stared indifferently at the supply center across the room. I didn't want him to see any traces of guilt in my eyes.

"As long as we have to do this stupid thing, we might as well try to make it somewhat painless," he went on. "We don't have to become best friends, but we can at least be professional."

I could feel my breath turn to steam. Was he calling me unprofessional? Just because I never went to some fancy art school?

"Fine!" I quickly stood and shouldered my backpack. "Go home and draw your sketches, and I'll do mine. We can meet here tomorrow morning and decide on the best one. That sound fair and *professional* to you?"

He stared at me for a few seconds. It looked like he almost wanted to smile. "Sounds cool to me," he said.

"Fine. Great. Won-der-ful," I said with phony enthusiasm. "I'll be here a half hour early."

I spun around and headed out the door, halfway conscious of him calling out some sarcastic good-bye.

God, what have I gotten myself into? I wondered. I could just imagine the awful avant-garde stuff he'd show up with the next day. Just my luck I'd end up doing the whole thing myself in order not to let down Ms. Crowley.

That is, if I didn't go insane first.

Cameron

Cameron, would you please move this box into my office? Could you please drive over to the rental place, Cameron, dear? Cameron, Cameron, Cameron . . .

I walked through the double French doors onto the terrace, pausing to catch my breath before continuing to the storage shed. Aunt Lenore had been relentless ever since I arrived at the country club after school. I was getting so sick of hearing her call me. The next time anyone said my name, I was likely to go ballistic.

"Cameron!" cried a different female voice.

I looked up to see Ashleigh waving at me from one of the wrought-iron deck tables. *Okay, scratch that. She* can *say my name anytime.*

"Come on over!" she said, motioning me toward her. I followed like a zombie.

"H-Hey," I stammered. "What are you doing here?"

She rolled her eyes. "I'm always here, unfortunately. I come by after school and do my homework while my dad plays golf."

"I see," I said, nodding and grinning like an imbecile. *She's here every day, huh?* I thought. *That changes my attitude about working here.*

"What about you?" she asked.

"I'm helping Aunt Lenore fix up the place for the pageant."

"Jeez, I'm sorry." She wrinkled her nose sympathetically. "I know you're sick of all this Fall Fest nonsense. Can you sit down a moment and talk?"

"Uh . . . sure." I glanced around for Aunt Lenore, but the coast was clear. Slowly, carefully, I pulled out the wrought-iron patio chair and sat down, trying not to seem too eager. I wondered if Ashleigh could tell how shaky I felt. On the one hand, I was totally jazzed about her talking to me, but on the other hand, I felt sort of unprepared. Never in my wildest dreams did I figure she and I could get so chummy in just two days.

"So . . . ," I began, ransacking my brain for a topic, "who do you think your dad will pick for grand marshal?"

"Beats me," she replied, shrugging. "Your cousin Blaine is really sucking up for the part. He's all but promised my dad his firstborn child."

"Really?" I asked. It figured. Blaine always did go for stuff like that. He probably dreamed about being grand marshal the way other guys dream about Katie Holmes.

"Hey, I know!" Ashleigh sat up straighter and whacked the table with the palm of her hand. "I should suggest *you* for grand marshal!"

"Me?" I squeaked.

"Why not?" she asked.

It was sweet—and surprising—of her to think of it. "I don't think so." I shook my head. "I'm not the right type. I'm too . . ."

"Shy?" she finished for me. "I think I know what you're saying." Suddenly she burst out laughing. "Hey, remember back in fourth grade? We made those cardboard mailboxes for Valentine's Day, and you put an anonymous heart-shaped box of chocolates in mine?"

My toes and fingers grew numb as the blood emptied out of them, racing upward to color my face. "But . . . how did you know it was me?"

Ashleigh grinned impishly. "Well, I only knew for certain this very moment. But I always assumed it was you. You were the only boy romantic enough to do something like that. And you were probably the only one who could spell *admirer* correctly."

I was too stunned to speak. During all those years of school I figured she barely knew who I was. Now I was finding out that she not only knew me, she knew my secrets as well.

"I kept waiting for you to reveal yourself, but you never did," Ashleigh went on. "Then I guess you set your sights on someone else."

My heart sloshed over with emotion. I wanted to tell her no. I never thought of anyone besides her. Even when I hooked up with Tamara Humes that one summer or Jenna Templeton last year, it was mainly because they went after me and I thought they were nice enough. But I never felt about them, or anyone, the way I felt about Ashleigh.

Words thundered through my mind. *Now's the time,* they said. *Ask her out!*

"Ash," I murmured, staring into her mesquite-colored eyes. "I—"

"There you are, honey!" a loud, male voice boomed across the terrace. I jumped about two inches out of my chair and jerked my head toward the noise. I could make out Mayor Witherspoon's burly outline against the setting sun.

He strode up to the table and sat down. His eyes squinted against the sunlight, and his wide, sun-burned face glistened with perspiration. "Whew! That was one lousy golf game! It was like someone with a mean sense of humor was controlling my ball!" He laughed the same laugh as Ashleigh's—only deeper and more deafening. Then he turned to me. "How you doin', sport?" he asked, clapping me on my shoulder.

"Fine, sir," I replied.

"Dad, this is Cameron Gallagher. He's in school with me," Ashleigh said. "Cameron, this is my dad."

"Gallagher?" he asked, scrunching up his eyes. "Oh, yes. Lenore's nephew, right?"

"Yes, sir."

"I should have known!" he said. "So, what're you kids up to? Studying?"

I could feel the heat rush to my face. There was no way I could ask Ashleigh out now. "Um, actually," I began, standing up, "I need to finish some chores for my aunt. It was nice meeting you, sir. See you at school, Ashleigh."

"Bye, son!" boomed Mayor Witherspoon.

Ashleigh flashed me a look of some sort. Apology? Pity? I couldn't tell. "See you," she said.

I turned and raced off toward the storage shed, my heart outpacing my feet. Guess I'd have to find some other opportunity to ask out Ashleigh. I just hoped when the time came, I'd get up the nerve to do it.

Official Federation Log of Doyle Jackowski.
Star Date 20.01.8.

*Interesting news on the academic front. Our crew seems to have found a new member. An alien of sorts and a true rarity in the universe: a beautiful girl who actually has a heart and brain.

*I can't help but feel the Force is at work here. Our mission is clear. We must dethrone the evil queen of the Empire and usher in a new age. One where intelligence counts more than athleticism, where principles are worth more than popularity, where brainiacs and beautiful people live in harmony . . .

*Or at least where someone can get elected festival queen who really deserves it.

Five

Cameron

I WAS SITTING in the kitchen, absently spooning Cheerios into my mouth and thinking about Ashleigh. More precisely, I was thinking about her for about the fiftieth time since I'd awakened. It killed me to think how close I'd come to asking her out the night before and then totally wimped out.

A noise made me look up. Blaine stood just inside the swinging doors to the kitchen. He was still in his underwear, and his sun-streaked hair stuck up all over, making him look like an overgrown Bart Simpson.

"I saw you," he said, a hint of a sneer in his tone.

"What are you talking about?" I asked.

He took a few steps forward and waggled his index finger at me. "I saw you at the club last night, talking to Ashleigh Witherspoon. *She's* the one you think you're gonna ask out, isn't she?"

I was glad I was sitting down because I suddenly felt shaky. There was no way I could look into Blaine's smirking face and effectively deny it. But there was no way I'd tell him the truth either. "None of your business," I said.

"Ha! I knew it!" he yelled triumphantly. "No way would she go out with you."

A mixture of anger and dread flooded my body, making me forget to play it cool. "Why not?" I asked.

Blaine sat down opposite me at the breakfast nook. "Cam, Cam, Cam." He shook his head, that smug smile still on his face.

Part of me wanted him to just disappear, to pop like a large bubble. But part of me wanted to hear him out. After all, Blaine had had tons of girlfriends. And he never seemed afraid to approach any girl in school. If he had a theory on my chances with Ash, I sort of wanted to know what it was.

"You're dreaming, dude," he said. "Ash is practically royalty. Her dad's the mayor. Not only that, but he's rich—even richer than me. You're the son of some grunt garage mechanic." He reached over and grabbed the box of Cheerios. Then he propped his bare feet on the table, reached into the box, and stuffed a giant handful of cereal into his mouth. "Having rich relatives doesn't make you worthy by association, cuz."

I couldn't handle it. I knew if I stayed in that kitchen a moment longer, I'd punch Blaine's nose into his sinus cavity.

Grabbing my half-eaten bowl of cereal, I quickly

stood and marched over to the sink. I hastily emptied my breakfast down the disposal, rinsed out my dish, and then headed for the door. Not exactly the dramatic exit most would have made, but that was me. Always the responsible Boy Scout.

I could hear Blaine cackling behind me as I barged through the kitchen doorway and headed into the foyer.

He's wrong! I kept telling myself as I walked out of the house and down the sidewalk toward the garage.

Blaine was just an ape. I knew Ashleigh had been giving me clear signals. At least, I thought she had. Fairly certain about it. Maybe.

Or was I just fooling myself?

Marissa

I paced around Ms. Crowley's room, far too angry to draw. If things weren't bad enough, all this time with Fry was messing with my art.

Last night I'd been so steamed at Fry, none of my backdrop sketches came out particularly well. I finally cranked out two rough ideas. One was an Old West theme, with a wagon wheel, a cow skull, and several large cacti. The other was a fairy-tale theme with a castle skyline. Definitely not my best work. But then, this wasn't exactly an inspiring assignment either.

"You here already?" Fry loomed in the doorway, balancing his motorcycle helmet on his hip. "Man, I thought I was early. I was going to sculpt while I waited." He pulled something out of his leather satchel, walked over to me, and shoved it into my hands. "This is what I came up with for the backdrop."

I rolled my eyes and looked down at what he'd handed me, half expecting some avant-garde scribble on the back of a cigarette carton. Instead I held a page of Arches paper with a finely detailed color drawing on it. And it was good! Incredible, in fact.

Fry had done a Texas landscape too, only his was much better than mine. The mesquite trees were zigzaggy brown lines and triangular green leaves. The scrub desert was different-colored wave patterns with bristly clumps of grass and a diamond-shaped cactus. There was even a cow skull. Unlike mine, though, Fry's was a Picasso-type rendering full of gray angles, long, spiky horns, and squarish holes for the eyes. But the best part was the sharp sliver of a moon and dozens of big, crooked stars floating over the whole thing.

"Wow," I whispered. There was no way I could come up with a sarcastic remark about this piece. And that bugged me to no end.

"Let me look at your stuff," he said.

I balked. How could I show him my lame drawings after this? He'd totally rag me out. And it was his fault they turned out so badly in the first place.

"Can't," I said, wrinkling my nose. "I forgot them at home. It's okay. They were too complicated anyway. Let's go with yours."

"You sure? Because yesterday you seemed all hopped up about—"

"I'm sure!" I snapped. I knew if we kept talking, I'd have to keep lying or explain myself. And I didn't want to do either. "Let's just get this over with."

"Fine with me," Fry said, running a hand through that tangle of hair. "Let's work." He loped over to a nearby table and sat down. His long legs stretched way out in front of him, revealing every tear in the front of his ratty jeans.

I sat down opposite Fry, placing his sketch in front of me. "Well, we can't really do anything until we have the measurements of the stage area," I said in what Mom would call my know-it-all voice. "So why don't you go by the country club after school today and—"

"No," he interrupted. "Why don't *you* go by the club and take measurements. I'll do a more detailed rendering."

"Why me?" I snapped. "Why can't I do the drawing? Do you think I'm not good enough or something?"

"Of course you're good enough," he said. "But those high-society people at the club will take one look at me and call security."

"Oh." Once again I totally backed down. I just couldn't win with the guy. Not only did he have an inarguable point about the club folks, but the calm, cool way he'd said "of course you're good enough" made me swallow my angry words in one gulp.

A knock sounded on the door, and a short, red-headed guy walked in, followed by six more nerdy-looking clones. The redhead, obviously their leader, carried a stack of papers in his hands. "Hey, guys. Do you want to fill out nominations for Fall Fest queen?" he asked.

"Like I care," I muttered.

"Sorry, dudes." Fry shook his head, causing his long bangs to swish in front of his face. "We've got more important stuff to do."

"It's for your sister," the redhead added.

"What?" Fry tossed back his head and laughed. "No way would Gwen go for that! Give it up, dude. Or she'll kill you if she finds out."

The redhead didn't seem the least bit fazed. "We think she's got the best chance of beating the 'in' crowd. People like her. She's intelligent, nice, not at all phony, and she's got the looks too."

A pudgy guy with glasses that made his eyes look big and scared whacked the redhead on his arm. *"Ixnay on the ookslay!"* he whispered. "Do you want to get us beat up?"

The redhead jabbed backward with his elbow, ignoring his buddy. "Anyway," he went on. "According to contest rules, each contestant needs to have ten independent nominations. The seven of us have filled out forms for her, but we need three more."

It was amazing to see how this little band of geeks had rallied around Gwen Darby. I knew exactly who she was—everyone did. When she and Fry first arrived, the town talked about how pretty and sophisticated she was almost as much as they talked about how scary Fry looked. For a while it looked like she was destined to become another Bree Hampton replica, but lately I'd noticed she'd distanced herself from them. Or vice versa.

"I'll do one," I said, leaping out of my seat to grab a paper. "Anything to shake up the status quo."

"Great," the redhead said. Then he turned back toward Fry. "What about you?"

"Are you kidding? I have to live with her. If she ever found out I helped make her do this, she'd make my life hell."

"But technically we aren't forcing her into this," the redhead countered. "All we're doing is nominating her. If she chooses not to run, she doesn't have to."

Fry seemed on the verge of caving for a second, but then he shook his head. "Naw, man. If she wants to run, she can ask me to fill out a form. Otherwise I'll stay out of it."

The redhead looked crushed, and all seven of them seemed to slump simultaneously. I had to admire Fry for sticking up for his sister, though. I never would have thought he'd have loyalty like that in him.

"Look," the redhead began again, his voice fast and urgent sounding. "One of the reasons we want her nominated is because she's the type who would never seek the nomination herself. Don't you see? We want her to be queen because she's not snotty enough to want it."

"Huh?" Fry asked.

"Please fill out a form. All we need to do is get her in. If she doesn't want it, she can back out. But I think we can convince her to do it. Just give us a chance. Please?" The guy gave Fry such a pleading look, I half expected him to fall on his knees. Even a few of the more timid ones were adding their own "pleases."

"Come on," I said to Fry. "Just fill out the form."

Fry glanced from the group to me and then back again. Finally he exhaled loudly and snatched a form out of the redhead's hands.

"Whatever," Fry said. "But I'm telling you, she's not going to like this."

"Thanks!" the redhead exclaimed. "And don't worry, you can trust us to tell her. We know how to handle it."

Gwenyth

"You did *what?*" My voice reverberated across the lunchroom, causing several curious stares. I didn't care, though. I was more concerned about the outrageous and, hopefully, false statement Doyle had just uttered.

Doyle waited until the onlookers went back to their own business before answering me. "I said, we nominated you for Fall Fest queen." He swallowed hard but continued to look me right in the eye.

"Why would you do that?" I wailed. "I thought we were friends!"

"We are!" he replied. The others nodded vigorously.

"Then why are you pulling a sick joke on me?"

"Just hear us out, okay?" Doyle clasped his hands together and cleared his throat. I could tell I was in for one of his overrehearsed debate-club speeches. "See, we think you would be the perfect person to represent our school—our town, really. You're the only one who deserves it."

"Are you trying to humiliate me?" I closed my eyes and sighed deeply. "Look. It was a sweet thought, but no thanks. No way would I put myself through that. Bree's got the thing locked up, and you know it." I took my frustration out on my lunch bag, crunching it up in my fist until it was as small and dense as a bullet.

"Gwen, the school needs someone to challenge Bree," Doyle said. "The only person who really wants her to win is her. Everyone else would rather see you as queen."

"Yeah, right." I snorted.

"It's true," Doyle insisted. "Isn't it, guys?" The rest of the gang nodded and muttered their affirmatives.

I held up my hand. "Uh-uh. No. Just because you guys think—"

"But it's not just us," Bennett chimed in. "Other people nominated you too."

"Oh yeah?" I asked. "Who?"

"Marissa Valdez," Bennett replied.

"Don't think I know her," I said. "Anyone else?"

Silence fell over the table.

"Aha! I thought so." I sat back and folded my arms across my chest. I should have known they were yanking my chain. I knew these guys were fantasy nuts, but this was ridiculous.

"Actually, there were two other nominations," Doyle said.

"Oh, really? Who?" I asked, daring him to lie to me.

"One was . . ." Doyle squirmed noticeably. ". . . your brother."

I blinked at him a few times and then burst out laughing. "Right. My brother. Good one, guys," I said between chuckles. Then I noticed how serious they looked. An ominous feeling spread over me. "No way! He'd never do that to me."

"He did," Doyle said, staring down at the table.

"I'll kill him!" I yelled, throwing my hands up into the air.

"He was only trying to help," Rom said.

"Yeah. And he really had to be convinced," Haskell added.

"*Convinced?*" I hissed. "Who, exactly, convinced him?"

The guys hung their heads guiltily—all except for Doyle, who glared at Haskell.

I threw my hands up over my eyes and shook my head. "I can't believe you guys! You had no right!"

"Don't be mad, Gwen," Terry said.

"We only did it to get more nominations," Larry explained. "We needed to have ten by this morning to make the deadline."

"Wait a minute." I uncovered my face and frowned at Larry. "But that only makes nine. You guys plus Marissa and my brother." A small wellspring of hope sprang up inside me. Could it be possible that these math and computer whizzes miscounted and I didn't make the cut after all?

"No, there's ten," Doyle said, smiling. He must have read my mind. "We went to the office to turn in the forms we had so far and the secretary said another one had been handed in for you just a few minutes before."

"Who did *that* one?" I asked, my anger resurfacing. It looked like I'd be adding another person to my hit list.

"She wouldn't say," Doyle replied. "But don't you see? That's proof that you're the one the school wants. You've got to run."

"No! No, no, no!" I hollered, leaping out of my seat.

I marched through the cafeteria and headed into a nearby rest room. Luckily the farthest stall was empty. I locked the door and sat on the toilet, resting my throbbing head against my knees.

Had it come to this? Spending my lunch hour hiding in the bathroom? I had definitely hit rock bottom.

I didn't care anymore if I wasn't popular or cool. I didn't care if Bree Hampton gossiped about me until she was gasping for breath. But just when I finally thought I found a group of people I could depend on, they turned on me too.

Suddenly my life stank worse than the air in this bathroom.

FALL FESTIVAL QUEEN-NOMINATION FORMS
Who are you nominating and why?

Rom Reddenbacher: Gwen Darby. Because she's nice and she's a Zelda fan.

Larry Strunk: Gwen Darby. Because she's not phony and she looks like Neve Campbell.

Terry Strunk: Gwen Darby. Because she can talk about stuff most girls don't like to talk about. Like classic Godzilla movies and UFOs.

Bennett Farley: Gwen Darby. Because she can quote Monty Python.

Haskell Pinkerton: Gwen Darby. Because she prefers Macintosh over Windows.

Oscar Beasley: Gwen Darby. Because she knows Captain Kirk kicks Picard's butt.

Doyle Jackowski: Gwen Darby. Because it's time the general public had one of their own in power. Because Gwen will stand for everyone, jock or geek, scholar or thug. Gwen is the people's choice. The obvious choice. The only choice.

Marissa Valdez: Gwen Darby. Because she's cool.

Brian Darby: Gwen Darby. Because she's cool and would never get mad at her brother when he's only trying to help.

Tony Etheridge: Gwen Darby. Because, um— Look, I can't say on this form, okay?

Six

Cameron

I STOOD AROUND the corner from the country club's terrace, peering through the branches of a crepe myrtle tree. Twenty yards in front of me Ashleigh sat at one of the patio tables, her head buried in her English textbook.

I wanted to go talk to her. I really did. But I was still bummed about what Blaine said that morning. What if he was right? On the one hand, I usually didn't even trust Blaine to give me the correct time of day. But on the other hand, my progress with Ashleigh lately *did* seem a little too good to be true.

Maybe I should just go talk to Ashleigh. If she seemed encouraging, great. If not, I'd feel like the biggest idiot on the continent, but at least I'd know for sure that I had no chance.

I took a deep breath and commanded my feet to take me to her table. "Hey," I said.

Ashleigh's head snapped up in surprise. "Hey!" she greeted with a warm smile. "How's it going? Still working hard on the pageant setup?"

"You wouldn't believe it." I sat down in the chair next to her—not because I felt all that confident, but because I didn't trust my feet to hold out while she smiled at me that way.

"Try me." She raised her eyebrows into two perfect semicircles, like the top part of a Valentine.

I sighed and shook my head. "Well, I think I've finally fumigated the place to her liking. There's not a speck of dust to be found."

"Good."

"The hardwood floors have been buffed, and the drapes have been dry-cleaned."

"Good."

"And all the mice have been fitted for tuxedos."

Ashleigh laughed musically, reaching over to push me lightly on the shoulder.

"Ashleigh, honey!" A deep voice echoed across the terrace. "Pull out a chair for your old man!" Mayor Witherspoon's hefty shape lumbered toward us. Beside him walked another figure carrying a golf bag. I recognized the square haircut and swagger immediately. It was Blaine.

"Hey, Dad," Ashleigh called out. "Don't tell me you lost again."

Mr. Witherspoon settled himself on the other side of Ashleigh and mopped his forehead with a handkerchief. "Honey, *lost* isn't the right word for it. Humiliated myself is more like it."

"That's not true, Mr. Witherspoon," Blaine said, taking the remaining chair. "You did fine out there."

Mr. Witherspoon shook his head. "That's a nice thing to hear from the next Tiger Woods, but I'm afraid I'm just too old to keep up with you. Maybe it's time I took up bingo like all the other old fogies in this town."

"Stop it, Dad," Ashleigh scolded. "You'll never give up golf, and you know it. They'll be carrying your lifeless form off the greens before you'd ever hang up your clubs."

"You're probably right, sweetheart," the mayor said, laughing. Then he glanced at me. "Hello, there, Cameron. How are you today?"

"Just fine, sir," I replied.

He tilted his head and rubbed his chin. "Why is it I never see you out there playing?"

"I . . . well . . . I don't really have that much time to play, sir. Aunt Lenore needs my help setting up for the pageant."

"Nonsense!" The mayor pushed aside my comment with his hand. "A young man like you needs time to unwind. Lenore can get someone else to help out for a spell while you join me for a game."

"Yeah," Ashleigh jumped in. "Why don't *you* help out your mother, Blaine?"

Ashleigh's suggestion took me by surprise, but I wasn't half as shocked as Blaine. His mouth dropped open, and his face lost all evidence of its usual smugness.

"I—I do help her out," he stammered. "I mean, I do it after I'm done training and everything. She knows how hard I need to practice if I want to make the tournament. Besides, Cam's better at the mechanical stuff. Right, Cam?"

Ashleigh and Mayor Witherspoon looked back toward me, giving Blaine a chance to shoot me a dirty look.

"Well . . . ," I began.

"Nonsense!" the mayor said again. "That doesn't mean you can't take a couple of hours and play a friendly game of golf. What do you say, Cameron?"

Again Blaine hardened his gaze at me. I didn't know what he was so mad at me for. I wasn't doing anything except sitting there.

"Thanks, Mr. Witherspoon. But as much as I'd like to, I really can't. I'm just not a golfer." I shrugged apologetically.

Blaine snorted. "I'll say. He thinks a drive is something a car does."

The mayor laughed heartily. I felt like I was collapsing inward from embarrassment. A few more cheap shots like that and there'd be a tiny black hole where I'd been sitting.

"Sounds like the sort of golfing partner I need." Mayor Witherspoon pushed back his chair and stood up. "Let me know if you change your mind about playing, okay?"

"Yes, sir," I replied.

The mayor clapped me on the back a couple of times and then turned toward Blaine. "Come on, ace. Let's go get that water I owe you."

They headed back through the French patio

doors toward the bar, Blaine flashing me one of his looks as he passed my chair. After they were gone, I couldn't even look at Ashleigh. My face was as red and hot as an enchilada.

"Sorry about that," she said. "My dad can come on kind of strong sometimes."

"It's all right," I mumbled. "Actually, I should leave too. I've got to finish up an errand." I jumped out of my seat and pushed the chair back under the table.

Ashleigh reached out and grabbed my arm. "Hang on a sec," she said. "You know, there's an assembly tomorrow on Fall Festival. Why don't we sit together? That way we could, you know, poke fun at the festival extremism and all."

My whole body seemed to lighten. She wanted to sit with me? In public? If this wasn't a good sign, I didn't know what was.

Marissa

Instead of walking home after school, I headed west to the Kingstown Country Club, a huge, red-brick compound covered with ivy.

Everyone who was anyone belonged to that club. That meant my dad, who served a few terms as a city councilman, was expected to have a membership. He was never real active, but he'd go there from time to time to play golf with Mayor Witherspoon or have lunch with some lawyer or just be seen. Occasionally I'd tag along to swim or—during

70

my boy-crazy days—scan for some of the local hunks. But it had been over a year since I'd set foot in the place. Ever since Dad's heart attack, he seemed to be avoiding coming here too. It was like he was embarrassed about having to admit weakness or something.

I patted the pocket of my black cargo pants to make sure the tape measure I borrowed from Ms. Crowley was still there. Then I walked through the heavy oak doors.

"Miss Valdez," greeted Henry, the club's security guard. "How's your father?"

"He's fine. Thanks." I always liked Henry. Besides being the spitting image of Danny DeVito, he was also the nicest person in that snooty place.

"Are your parents going to join you for dinner?" he asked.

I shook my head. "No. I'm here by myself. I just need to take some measurements of the stage area. Which way is the ballroom?"

"That way, past the bar," he said, pointing.

I thanked him and had headed in that direction when someone called my name. I looked over and saw Will Benson leaning against the long, wooden bar, talking with Blaine Gallagher. They looked like bookends in khaki shorts. Both of them held bottles of fizzy water and wore matching little self-satisfied grins on their faces.

"What are you doing here?" Will asked me. "Looking for someone?"

I could tell by his tone he was referring to himself. *Dream on,* I thought. "I've got work to do," I said, continuing toward the ballroom.

A second later Will and Blaine fell into step on either side of me. "Why don't we join you?" Will said. "I'm finished with my tennis game, and Blaine just beat the mayor at golf."

"Whoop-de-do," I muttered.

"Where are you headed?" Will asked.

I sighed impatiently. "I need to measure the stage area for the backdrop we're making."

"Then we really should go with you. Club rules don't permit people in closed rooms unless accompanied by an employee," Blaine announced.

"That's right," Will remarked in a serious tone while slapping Blaine's hand behind my back.

I stopped walking and shot Will a dirty look. "You don't work here."

"He doesn't," Blaine cut in. "But I do."

"Right." I snorted. "Since when do you work?"

Will thought that was funny, but Blaine didn't. "Don't get all stuck up with me," he said. "My mom just locked the ballroom before my cousin drove her home. Now *I'm* the only one with a key." He smiled smugly and held up a wad of keys suspended on a leather BMW key chain.

"Whatever," I said, rolling my eyes. "Could you please just let me in there? I want to get these stupid measurements and go home."

Blaine unlocked the doors to the ballroom and switched on the lights. A golden glow immediately filled the room, as if the place were covered in fairy

72

dust. I stood and cocked my head at the stage, trying to imagine how it would look with the backdrop. Then I mounted the side steps and began measuring the area.

"So you're doing the backdrop, huh?" Will called out. "Need any help?"

"No thanks. I've got a partner," I replied tersely. I pulled a pencil and piece of paper out of my book bag and wrote down the length we needed.

"Really?" Will sat on the edge of the stage and leaned back on his hands. "Who is it?"

"Fry Darby," I answered while gauging the depth of the area.

Will and Blaine burst out laughing. "No way!" Blaine exclaimed. "*That* burnout?"

"Man, I feel sorry for you!" Will shook his head.

Blaine sat down on the stage a few feet from Will. "*That* is one weird dude," he said.

"No kidding," Will added. "You get a load of the guy's hair? Looks like an armadillo's nest."

"Yeah." Blaine chortled. "And he probably gets those clothes from that thrift store on Rio Grande Street."

I silently wrote down measurements and tried to ignore their idiotic comments as best I could. I considered pointing out that someone who deviated from the preppy uniforms they wore wasn't automatically a weirdo. And I still didn't know Fry very well, but I did know he wasn't a total brain-dead freak. Not if he could do art as well as he could. But I kept my mouth shut and let them ramble on. It wasn't like they'd believe me anyway.

"So what's it like working with Fry, Marissa?" Will asked.

I shrugged and started throwing stuff back into my backpack. "Like nothing. It's just a dumb project." I wished they would just get a clue and leave me alone.

"Aren't you kind of scared?" Blaine asked. "I mean, what if he flips out and tries to strangle you or something?"

I stared at Blaine and shook my head, amazed at the complete lack of any higher intelligence the guy possessed. It was a miracle he could walk. "You're wigging," I said. "Fry's not like that."

"Oh, really?" Will asked in a singsongy voice. "What? You like him? Is that why you're partners?"

I closed my eyes and pressed my fingertips to my temples. Suddenly I was surrounded by preschoolers. "Look, it wasn't my idea to work with him. I'm only tolerating the guy to make an A in Crowley's class. And I'm not some crybaby who's going to whine myself out of it just because the guy looks scary."

Actually, I *had* tried to whine myself out of it. But there was no reason they needed to know that.

"Well, let us know if he starts bugging you," Will said. "We'll make the guy suffer. Right, Blaine?"

"Yeah. Like, we'll make him take a bath."

The two of them cracked up, slapping high fives and howling like chimpanzees. I gathered my things as quickly as I could and strode out of there.

What jerks! For some reason, all the guys around here had the personalities of baboons.

It was clear if I ever wanted to settle down with a guy, I'd have to look elsewhere. Like Mars, maybe.

Gwenyth

"All right, you've got five minutes!" I stood in my brother's doorway, yelling at the top of my lungs. Our folks were still at work, so I could be as loud as I wanted.

Brian barely looked up. It was as if he'd been expecting me. "Five minutes? For what?"

"To explain why you felt it necessary to nominate me for queen bimbo!"

"Oh, that," he said, bending back over his sketch pad. "You heard, huh?"

"Yes, I heard! Five minutes! Then I start removing your limbs!" I marched into his room and slammed the door behind me. The noise reverberated throughout our old wooden bungalow house. Having been raised in cramped New York apartments, I couldn't get used to having a whole house—and yard. It almost felt like too much space at times. That combined with the expansive Texas horizon often made me feel woozy.

"What's the big deal?" he asked, still sitting cross-legged on his bed, drawing.

His composure only made me madder. "I hate stuff like that, and you know it! It's bad enough that we had to move here. But now this? Just when I thought I could blend in and become another anonymous face, you have to enter me in this stupid contest!"

I stalked over to the bed and hollered right over him, waving my arms like some crazed orchestra conductor. Brian at least stopped sketching and looked up, but his casual expression never changed.

"You're my brother!" I continued ranting. "You're supposed to stand up for me and protect me! Instead you pull this prank!" My voice crumbled into a whine, and I slumped down onto his denim bedspread. "Why are you doing this to me?"

Brian pushed his long bangs out of his face. "I didn't do it *to* you. I did it *for* you," he explained. "When those dudes came into the art room and asked me to nominate you, I first told them to get lost. But then I thought of something."

"What?" I asked.

"I thought about you." He set down his sketch pad and scooted around to face me. "I thought about all those times you yelled at me to take a stand. Back at Reese you were always trying to get me to sign up for this or march for that and show up at some meeting. And just the other day you were telling me I should try to get more involved and give this place a chance. Well, guess what. This is *your* chance."

I shook my head. "Don't turn the tables on me. This is totally different."

"No, it isn't," he countered. "The only way to shake the system in this place is to do it internally. You've got a chance to challenge those snobs head-on.

You can either try to completely avoid those people for the rest of the school year or you can show them outright that you aren't afraid of them. I always figured you'd choose the latter."

"But I . . . ," I started to argue. Only it was more of a reflex than anything. I had nothing to say, and he knew it.

Brian slid off the bed and headed for the door. "Besides," he said, stepping into the hallway. "I think you deserve to be queen. And I think you can win."

FROM THE DESK OF LENORE GALLAGHER

Things to do for pageant:
　　—Get programs printed. ~~Blaine~~ Cameron
　　—Buff hardwood floors. ~~Blaine~~ Cameron
　　—Check sound system. ~~Blaine~~ Cameron
　　—Fix lighting. ~~Blaine~~ Cameron
　　—Have drapes dry-cleaned. ~~Blaine~~ Cameron
　　—Set up chairs. ~~Blaine~~ Cameron
　　—Set up podium and risers. ~~Blaine~~ Cameron
　　—Get tiara cleaned. Me

Seven

Marissa

MOM PLUNKED A football-sized omelette in front of me. "You need to eat," she said. "Right, Ernesto?"

Dad grunted affirmatively from behind his paper.

I rolled my eyes, angry with myself for sleeping too late to avoid them with the have-to-get-to-school-early excuse. All night I had tossed and turned with bad dreams. Weird ones where I was stuck in a zoo cage with Fry Darby—only he was this big, fanged gorilla instead of himself—and Will Benson and Blaine Gallagher stood on the other side of the bars, laughing and throwing popcorn at us.

This stupid project is making me lose my mind, I thought, taking a big slurp of coffee. All I needed was to get through the morning small talk with Mom and Dad and endure seven hours of brain-petrifying classes and stomach working with Fry for an hour or two after school. Then I could come home and crash.

"So how's your art coming along?" Mom asked, sitting in the empty chair beside me.

I sighed loudly and closed my eyes, trying to shut out the world. Looked like I wouldn't even get through the small talk.

Maybe if I'd had more than three hours of real sleep, I would have been stronger. Or maybe if I'd already finished one full cup of coffee, I could have been quick enough to sidestep the issue. Instead I felt all my defenses crumple like a paper napkin.

"I'm not working on my stuff right now," I whined. Just thinking about my sketch filled me with frustration. And it wasn't just having to put off working on it that upset me. The scary part was that even when I was working on it, I hadn't been doing a very good job.

Dad lowered his paper and frowned at me suspiciously. "Then why have you been getting to school early and staying late?"

An uneasy feeling jump-started my heart, like a giant jolt of caffeine. I could tell when Dad was x raying my life. The best thing to do was to play it cool. "Ms. Crowley has me doing something different," I mumbled, pulling my eyes away from his. "A backdrop for the Fall Fest queen pageant."

"No wonder you're so tired!" my mother exclaimed. "Ms. Crowley shouldn't expect you to take on such a large project all by yourself! Maybe I should call her and—"

"No!" I cried. "I'm not doing it by myself. Some-one's helping me."

I tried to say it as casually as possible. I really did. But Dad must have sensed some hesitation in my voice.

"Who are you working with?" he asked.

I paused, wondering if I should just lie to him. But if he called Ms. Crowley and found out the truth, I'd be in major trouble. Might as well spare myself the suspense and face things now. "Fry Darby," I replied as nonchalantly as I could.

"What?" Dad's face turned the color of cran-berry juice. "What is that woman thinking? How dare she make you work with that criminal!" In one swift movement he pushed back his chair and sprang upright, heading for the wall phone.

"Dad! What are you doing?" I asked. I was so afraid. Afraid of what he might do and afraid of what all this might do to him.

"I'm calling the school," he said, wrenching the receiver from its post. "They're putting a stop to this now, or you're dropping out of art."

"No!" I shouted, jumping out of my chair.

Dad narrowed his eyes at me, but at least he stopped pushing buttons. I took a deep breath and tried to control the emotion in my voice.

"Dad, it's okay. I don't need your help," I said, choosing my words carefully. "You know how much art means to me. And Ms. Crowley has been so great, letting me use her supplies and use the room before and after school. This is the least I can do to pay her back. Please, Dad. Just trust me on this."

Dad moved his index finger away from the phone and shook it toward me. "I don't want you having to work with that . . . that *person,*" he said, spitting out the last word as if it were an awful curse. But I noticed his voice had lost a little of the anger.

"I can take care of myself, Dad," I went on. "I promise. And I promise I won't work with Fry unsupervised. Okay?"

There was a long pause. Mom looked from him to me and back again.

"Please, Ernesto," she said. "It means a lot to her."

I wanted to reach over and thank my mom, but I was afraid to move. I could tell he was caving, and I was scared any sudden movement on my part might snap him out of it.

"Okay," he said finally. He replaced the phone receiver and turned to face me again, his eyes wide and serious. "But if I hear about that kid doing anything wrong—I mean *anything*—you are going to stop this project even if you have to quit the class. Understand?"

"I understand," I replied, trying to assure him with the confidence in my voice. Inside, though, I didn't felt so sure about things.

Could I really trust Fry not to screw up during this project? What if he got caught doing something stupid and I had to drop out of art—all because of him?

No, I told myself. *Fry might be weird, but he's not dumb. Besides, when it comes to art, he's almost professional. He'll come through.*

He has to.

"We all know this student body will behave respectfully during this year's Fall Festival," Principal Sullivan was saying into the microphone. In front of him five hundred students squirmed, stared at their nails, or talked to each other in hushed tones.

Tiffany Anderson, who sat on the other side of Ashleigh, was one of the talkers.

"Respectfully." She snorted. "Yeah, right. They ought to give out blue ribbons for wishful thinking."

"Thanks to your efforts," Principal Sullivan went on, "we are sure to have one of the best festivals ever—full of fun and surprises."

"Oh, sure. Lots of surprises." Tiffany grimaced so hard, I thought all that makeup she wore might burst off in a powdery cloud. "Like the big mystery of who the next Fall Fest queen will be. I mean, really. The whole town knows Bree Hampton will win. They ought to just toss her the crown right now and spare us the stupid pageant. Right, Ash?"

"Maybe so," Ashleigh whispered, sneaking me an apologetic look. I could tell she was just as fed up with Tiffany's ramblings as I was, but she was too polite to tell her to can it.

I, on the other hand, was seriously considering whether I could squeeze the air out of Tiffany's throat without anyone noticing—or caring. All last night and this morning I had been looking forward to the assembly. A whole hour of sitting next to Ashleigh sounded like pure bliss. I figured we'd get the chance to talk some more, and maybe, if the perfect moment presented itself, I'd get up the nerve to ask her out.

Instead Tiffany took it upon herself to fall in step with Ash and me while our class walked to the auditorium. Then she plopped down on the bleachers next to Ashleigh as if her name had been stenciled on it. Now, even if I could get a word in edgewise, I couldn't ask Ash out. Not with one of the school's biggest blabbermouths within earshot.

"God, I hope we get some decent people at the dance this year," Tiffany went on. "Last year it was the lamest of the lame. Don't you think?"

"Mmmm," Ashleigh replied.

"Ugh!" Tiffany exclaimed, making another face. "I'm so sick of the guys in this town. I really hope some of the guys from Farhills show up. I met this one guy over the summer—he was such a cutie!" She leaned toward Ashleigh, and I could see the dreamy-eyed look on her face. "His name is Wayne—or maybe it was Dwayne. Anyway, unlike the rodeo clowns around here, he knows what real style is. I don't think he even owns a pair of cowboy boots, and his Skechers looked new. No holes or dirt clods."

I suddenly felt really uncomfortable. As Tiffany blathered on, I became hyperaware of my own dusty Reeboks and the faded spots on the knees of my jeans. Did girls really care about that stuff? I watched as Ashleigh nodded along to what Tiffany was saying. Was she just being polite? Or did she agree with her?

"I mean, this guy was quality," Tiffany continued.

"He really knew how to take care of himself. Most guys can't understand why girls wouldn't want to hold hands with someone who has calluses and dirt under his nails."

I squirmed like my seat had needles sticking out of it. I considered sitting on my hands, but I thought that would be too obvious. After eight years of helping my dad fix cars, I'd gotten some major calluses. I'd never really thought about it before, but my hands did look like big, rough paws. Probably felt that way to the touch too. At least my nails were clean, if that helped any.

"What do you think, Ash?" Tiffany asked. "You want me to see if Wayne has any cool friends?"

Ashleigh seemed taken aback. "Well . . . not really." She glanced sheepishly at me.

Tiffany leaned forward, following her gaze, and I could tell by her wide-eyed expression that she'd finally gotten a clue about the two of us sitting together.

"Never mind, Ash," Tiffany said, sitting back upright. Then, for the first time since we'd left Mrs. Langtree's classroom, she shut up.

All of a sudden it was too quiet. Ashleigh smiled shyly at me, and I got the sense that both girls were waiting for me to say or do something. But what? Now that my situation had been made totally obvious to Tiffany, anything that happened from this point on would be superscrutinized.

Just at that moment there was a smattering of applause. "Now, here to name the contestants in the Fall Fest queen pageant is Mrs. Lenore Gallagher," Principal Sullivan announced.

I don't remember ever being so glad to see Aunt Lenore. As soon as she stepped up to the microphone, Tiffany and practically everyone else turned their attention to her.

I cupped my hand around my mouth and whispered into Ashleigh's ear, "I need to go now. I'm supposed to meet Aunt Lenore backstage and drive her to the club as soon as she's finished talking. Her car's still not fixed."

"Oh," Ash said slowly. "I'll see you later, right? At the club?"

"Maybe so," I replied, sidestepping my way down the bleachers. "I've got a lot of things to do first, though."

Like go buy some new hands, for one.

Gwenyth

Here it comes, I thought. My fists tightened, and my feet bounced at drumroll speed.

The lady in the red dress gripped the microphone lightly in her manicured fingertips, as if it were a cracker she was about to bite into. I figured she must be someone important to have five hundred antsy teenagers give her their undivided attention. Even Doyle, who sat two rows in front of me, stopped fiddling with his PalmPilot as soon as she hit the stage.

I tried to follow what she was saying, but I was too nervous. A lot of hokey stuff about "tradition" and "privilege" was all I could gather.

Just get to the point, I thought. *Name the nominees and get it over with.*

Doyle looked back at me but turned around as soon as I caught his eye. Since I stormed away from the lunch table yesterday, I hadn't said a word to him. I knew he thought I was still mad at him. I wasn't, but I figured I'd let him stew a little more. Maybe that would teach him not to interfere in my life without asking.

"The nominees for this year's Fall Festival queen pageant are . . ." The woman glanced down at a paper in her hand. Everyone in the place collectively leaned forward. ". . . a wonderful group of young women," she continued. "Any of whom would make an ideal queen."

Aaaugh! I screamed mentally. *I can't take much more!* The anticipation of hearing my name called out in front of everyone was starting to make me nauseous.

"As you know, the young woman who is chosen to be queen should possess the fine qualities of poise, talent, respectability, patience. . . ."

I tuned her out. If I was going to survive this suspense, I had to think about something else or go nuts. I was absently scanning the bleachers when something on my left caught my eye. There was someone watching me.

It was Tony. He was sitting several yards down and a couple of rows up, but he was clearly staring at me. Not only that, but he was smiling—a slight, almost secretive smile, like the kind you'd flash to your best friend when you're sharing a silent joke.

Just what my insides didn't need.

He looked great too. His brown hair rippling around his face like a fancy border, his green T-shirt lighting up his eyes and accenting his tanned, muscular arms as he leaned forward. For several seconds I literally could not pull my gaze away from him. Finally I realized how dorky I was being and turned away.

He's just a player, I kept telling myself. *Get over it.*

But I had been telling myself that for a few days now, and my brain either refused to believe it or was too busy cranking out saliva over him. It was weird. I'd never flipped over a guy like this—even in New York, where I'd dated a lot. Maybe I was just too lonely and frustrated to think straight, but I had to admit there was a part of me—a sappy, soap-opera-fed part of me—that felt drawn to Tony. As if in fate's grand scheme of things, *he* was the reason I ended up here.

I shook my head, trying to jar that thought loose. I didn't even know Tony. I was simply *attracted* to him. But attracted to the point that I *did* feel like I knew him. Did that even make sense?

"I would now like to read the names of this year's nominees," the fancy lady announced. A total, almost supernatural silence fell over the place. I held my breath.

"Tracy Reed."

A squeal came up from the audience—probably Tracy herself—followed by light applause.

"Linda Loftin."

Instinctively I glanced over at Linda's section. She blushed severely while those around her gave her congratulatory pats and shoves.

The lady named four other girls I didn't know. Each time a cheer would rise up from a particular section of the audience, followed by the standard amount of clapping.

"Bree Hampton," the lady called next.

A slightly louder cheer rose up. I spotted Bree just a couple of rows ahead of me to the right. She dropped her mouth open wide and touched her fingertips to her collarbone in a who-me? type of gesture. I couldn't believe she had the nerve to act surprised. Especially considering she already had her evening gown and was putting the finishing touches on her talent routine.

"And our last nominee is . . ." The lady looked down at her paper. The tightness in my chest grew so strong, I feared I might explode into tiny pieces. ". . . Gwenyth Darby!" she called at last.

I smiled, more out of nervousness than anything else, and glanced down at my shoes. I couldn't bear to look at the other students. Especially Tony. There was a respectable amount of applause, but I could hear someone behind me say, "Who's that?"

"The first round of the contest will begin at the club three days from now," the lady in red continued. "Those who choose not to accept the nomination should contact me right away. Thank you."

And then it was over. Principal Sullivan instructed everyone to go to their second-period classes, and the auditorium broke out into chaotic confusion. I remained in my seat while everyone tromped down the bleachers and out the nearest double doors.

The stream of departing students parted around Doyle, who stood rooted in his spot. After a minute or so, he approached. "So . . . what are you going to do?" he asked hesitantly.

I sighed and looked past him. I'd been asking myself that question for twelve straight hours. In New York, I would have never even considered such a thing. That wasn't me. Our school had lots of competitions within our field of study, but nothing as ludicrous as a beauty contest. Still, I couldn't stop thinking about what Brian said the night before—about taking on a challenge and standing up to the reigning establishment. That *was* me. Or at least, that was how I'd been in New York.

The gym was almost empty now, but Bree Hampton and her clones were huddled together, whispering and glancing at me. A chorus of snickering welled up from the group, and Bree lifted a cold gaze in my direction.

Suddenly it was as if a switch had been thrown, and my old cool, determined self—the New York me—came out of her hiding place.

"I'm going to do it," I said to Doyle, turning to meet his stunned stare. "I'm going to accept the nomination."

Online Conference

Doyle: Guys, I have some serious news. Gwen has decided to run for queen after all.

Rom: All right!

Larry: Cool!

Haskell: I knew she would!

Bennett: You did not!

Terry: What made her change her mind?

Doyle: I don't know. But forget that. We have lots of work to do!

Oscar: Like what?

Doyle: We've got to help Gwen win the contest. We got her into this, and we're going to make sure she wins. She's going to meet us at the library tomorrow night at six.

Bennett: Okay.

Haskell: I'll be there.

Rom: Ditto.

Larry: Me too.

Oscar: Count me in.

Terry: Okay. But when we're done, can we do some gaming?

Eight

Gwenyth

I WAS LATE. Since Mom and Dad were working every evening at the college, I'd tried to cook dinner. I figured, how hard could sloppy joes be? Answer? Harder than you'd think. I burned the sauce, burned the buns, and almost set fire to our kitchen.

So there I was, half starved, twenty minutes late to meet the guys, and with a large tomato sauce stain on my shirt that I discovered on the drive to the library. *What more could go wrong?* I wondered. Answer?

Bam! I rushed through the entrance and instantly collided with someone carrying a stack of books. I fell backward onto the tile floor of the foyer. The person tripped over my feet and landed beside me. Large, hardback volumes went flying in all directions, one of them bouncing off my head.

"Ow!" I cried, rubbing my forehead.

"Ow!" cried the person lying beside me. He sat up and glanced around in bewilderment before his eyes rested on me.

The way my luck had been going, I should have known it would be Tony Etheridge.

"You," he said simply.

"I'm so sorry," I said, reaching around to retrieve some of his fallen books.

"No, I'm the one who should be sorry," he said, rubbing the back of his neck.

I started to stand up, and Tony reached down, grabbed my hands, and pulled me upright. The movement was so fast and smooth, it almost made me dizzy. And the strength I sensed behind Tony's muscular arms didn't help either. Could a guy be any cuter?

"So, um, like I said . . . I'm sorry about this," I said, smoothing my shorts and blouse.

"Hey, no big deal. Fact is, I've been trying to think of reasons to talk to you, and this just spares me the trouble," Tony went on. He smiled. "See, you've totally thrown me off my game. All these times I try talking to you, you don't seem very, um, interested."

Thrown off my game? His words stabbed their way into the logical section of my brain. Just because I wasn't falling for his ultrasmooth plays, the guy was in some crisis?

"Let me try again," he said. He took a deep breath and opened his arms. "Would you like to go out to a movie sometime?"

Again, just like at the assembly, I could feel a dippy,

weak-kneed part of me inside, squealing with delight. But the rest of me stomped her into submission.

"No," I said coolly. "I don't think so."

Tony's face fell, and his arms drooped to his sides.

Before he could say anything further, I pushed open one of the glass doors leading into the library and quickly strode inside.

I didn't look back to see his reaction, and even if he'd said anything, I probably wouldn't have heard it the way my heart was thundering in my ears. As much as I liked looking at the guy, I wished he would just lay off. All the physical reactions he triggered had to be bad for my health.

"Gwen! There you are!" Doyle called from one of the tables. The rest of the gang sat around him.

"*Shhh!*" went some woman with a big, round Betty Rubble–type hairdo from behind the counter.

Doyle rolled his eyes and silently motioned me over.

"Sorry I'm late," I whispered as I reached the table. "What's up?"

"We've got a problem," Doyle announced gravely. "They always do the first round of eliminations in the pageant with a test."

"A test?" I asked.

"It's always a few days before the show. Mrs. Gallagher tests all the girls on their knowledge of Kingstown history, and the top five scorers make it to the show as semifinalists," Doyle explained.

"Oh, great," I said, dropping into an empty seat. "Why didn't you tell me? I've only lived here two and a half months. I barely know my address."

"Look, believe it or not, most teenagers around here don't give a flip about the town history," Doyle went on. "The contestants just study for it."

"Yeah," Haskell jumped in. "All you need to do is read the book."

"The book?" I asked.

Doyle nodded. "It's called *A Brief History of Kingstown*. It was written by some lady whose great-grandfather was one of the town's founding fathers."

"We wanted you to come here and study it, but it's all gone," Bennett said, his face all wide-eyed and worried looking.

"What do you mean, it's all gone?" I asked.

"It's really weird," Rom said, rubbing his chin thoughtfully. "They usually have twenty copies here, more than enough for all the nominees. But the librarian just told us they're all checked out."

"Then Haskell ran down to the bookstore, but they're out too," Larry added. "They won't get another shipment in for two weeks."

I sighed. "Well, maybe this is for the best. Maybe I should just quit." Part of me felt relieved, but surprisingly I was disappointed too. I had just started to get fired up about the contest—and the possibility of rattling Bree.

"No, don't," Doyle said. "There's still another way."

The other guys frowned in bewilderment.

"What?" Terry asked.

"There's us." Doyle smiled and swept his arm in

a circle. "We're going to tell Gwenyth everything we know about Kingstown."

Marissa

A handmade sign taped to the door of Wally's Paint, Hardware, and Sporting Goods Shop read, Gone to Post Office. Back in Ten Minutes.

"Man, that never happens in New York," Fry grumbled. "It would take a serious act of terrorism to shut down a place during business hours."

"Yeah?" I said, feeling steamed—although I was actually more embarrassed at our having to wait. "Well, at least we don't have traffic jams, smog, or gangs selling drugs outside the elementary school."

Fry smiled. "Didn't realize you were so in love with this place."

"I'm not! I just don't want you to assume we're backwoods hicks who think running water is a luxury."

"Maybe you shouldn't assume New York is a giant junkyard with criminals lurking behind every corner."

He had me there. "I don't think that," I said. "And I know more about New York than you think. Or at least I know about your old school, Reese." I sighed and plopped down on the sidewalk, leaning against the store's outer wall. "For years I dreamed about going someplace like that."

Fry looked at me strangely, half frowning, half smiling. *Great. Why'd I have to go and say that? Now he'll just make fun of me until I end up hitting him.*

"You'd love it there," he said, sitting Indian style on the sidewalk, facing me. "And you'd fit right in too."

I stared at him, completely stunned. I felt like I'd just been paid an incredible compliment. Suddenly Fry wasn't just this weirdo I was stuck working with; he was a link to a life I might have had—in some parallel universe.

"Tell me about it," I said. "About Reese."

Fry stared off toward a group of oak trees, only it was clear he wasn't really seeing them. His eyes looked far off, almost wistful. "It was the coolest place," he said, his voice low and thoughtful. "Nobody cared what you said or did. All that mattered was your art. And no one ever asked you to do something as stupid as paint a beauty-contest backdrop."

"Sounds like heaven," I mumbled.

Fry looked back at me as if he'd been surprised to hear my voice. "It wasn't perfect. I mean, there were jerks there. And people could be insanely competitive. But at least everyone there felt like they *belonged*."

He gazed off toward the trees again, his face sad. Again he struck me as being different. His wry smile and indifferent stare were gone. And except for the wild hair and grungy clothes, he seemed totally normal. Maybe even more . . . *gentle* than most.

"You kids waiting on me?" Wally Shepherd rounded the corner and walked up to the store.

"Yes, sir," I said, leaping to my feet. Fry quickly jumped up too, looking startled.

"Well, hi, there, Marissa," Mr. Shepherd said. "Didn't recognize you right off. How's your daddy feeling?"

"Fine, sir. Thank you."

"Y'all go on and help yourself to whatever you need," Mr. Shepherd said, unlocking the door and pushing it open for us. We snagged a cart and wended our way over to the back wall.

"So," Fry said, holding up a color-sample card. "What did he mean about your father?"

"My dad had a heart attack a while back. He's still recovering." *Physically* and *mentally,* I thought.

Fry looked right into my eyes. "I'm sorry. That's got to be rough." His voice was so sincere sounding, I couldn't reply. In fact, I could feel a lump forming in my throat. I suddenly realized that no one my age had really said that to me since it happened.

Before I could get all misty, I started filling the cart with gallons of paint. Soon we had a giant stack. "I think we've got what we need," I said.

Fry waved his finger over the cart, counting to himself. "Nah. We need more blue. There's probably some down here." He stooped way over and started rummaging along the bottom shelf.

All of a sudden Will Benson and Lenny Pipkin rounded the corner of the aisle. "Look who we have here," Will said. "What are you up to, Marissa?"

"Nothing," I replied. But just as I said that, Fry popped up and dropped two more buckets of blue paint into our cart. He eyed Will warily.

"Whoa," Will exclaimed. "Marissa, you didn't tell me you got a dog."

"Yeah," Lenny echoed. "I can't believe Wally let you bring him in here."

Will turned toward Fry. "What are you doing here, Burnout? Robbing the place?"

"I wouldn't talk, Cowboy," Fry said calmly. "You guys look like you're getting ready for a street fight."

It was true. Will carried a heavy steel chain, and Lenny had a crowbar and a giant wrench in his hands.

"We're working on my car, that's all!" Lenny spat.

Will grinned coldly and lifted his chin at Fry. "Course, you're probably an expert on street fights. Aren't you, Fryin'?"

"Sure. But I wouldn't mess with those things," Fry said, pointing at the chain in Will's arms. He grabbed an aluminum baseball bat off a nearby sporting-goods display and waved it in Will's face. "Personally, I prefer something like this. It makes such a nice thunk sound."

It was really creepy. Fry smiled mysteriously as he danced the bat under Will's nose. Part of me was afraid he might actually give us a demonstration. But part of me also loved seeing Will's conceited smile disappear, replaced by wide-eyed terror.

"Come on, Lenny," Will mumbled, keeping his eyes on Fry. "Let's go. This place is full of nutcases."

They disappeared around the corner of the aisle. Soon we heard the front-door chimes ring out as they left.

Fry made a *tsk-tsk* noise. "Shame. And it's only fourteen ninety-nine," he remarked, setting the bat on a shelf. "Sorry about that," he said, looking normal again. "I get that crap from people all the time. I wish they'd just leave me alone."

"I don't think you need to worry about them anymore. I thought Will was going to wet his pants." I laughed nervously.

Fry didn't even crack a smile. "Yeah, well . . . in New York, I learned that if people think you're stark raving, they usually stay away." He cocked his head and looked at me suspiciously. "You know, I really was faking to get those guys off my back. I'm not a lunatic for real."

I stared back at him. His forehead was all bunched up and his mouth twisted up sideways. He didn't look insane at all. In fact, he seemed almost concerned. *About what I might think of him?*

"Don't worry," I said, smiling. "I know you're not a lunatic."

Now if I could just convince my dad.

Cameron

Once again I had my head under the hood of Aunt Lenore's Beemer, only this time I was in the shade of the country club's pecan trees. I finally got the belt I needed and was able to attach it after school. Now I just wanted to go over everything and make sure it was safe. Then I could surprise Aunt Lenore.

In a way, it felt good to be tinkering with a car engine again. The whiff of motor oil, the pings and clangs of the tools, the warm, weighty feel of engine parts. That sort of stuff I could do. To fix cars, all you had to do was replace what was broken, refill what was low or empty, or reconnect anything that had come loose. It wasn't easy work, but it made sense. Unlike everything else in life.

After one last check of my repair I jumped into the driver's seat and started up the engine. I could tell by the way it sounded that it was fixed—the perfect pitch and intensity.

"Oh, my! Cameron, dear, did you fix it?" I turned and saw Aunt Lenore trotting across the parking lot with Blaine moseying along behind her.

"Yes, ma'am," I replied, stepping out of the car.

"Oh, Cameron! You're a savior!" Aunt Lenore reached up and tugged at both of my cheeks. "Blaine, dear! Isn't it wonderful?"

"Sure," he said, smirking in my direction. "It only took him most of the week."

My hand tightened around my wrench, and I briefly enjoyed an image of dismantling Blaine's facial features with it. I wanted to remind him the part took five days to arrive, which wasn't my fault, and I had to recharge the battery overnight. But it was no use trying to change his opinion.

"Now, Blaine," Aunt Lenore scolded. "It isn't nice to point out people's faults."

Right at that moment a shiny gold Lexus pulled

up alongside us. The tinted windows lowered, revealing Mayor Witherspoon's doughy face. I could see Ashleigh sitting next to him. She saw me and waved, her wide smile lighting up her face like a coat of Armor All.

I waved back, intensely aware of my dirty fingernails and sweat-stained shirt. Ever since Tiffany's little sermon on personal hygiene yesterday morning, I'd been really self-conscious about my looks.

"What are you people doing out in the heat?" Mayor Witherspoon demanded. "Blaine, don't tell me your ball flew out here into the parking lot?"

Blaine laughed loudly. "No, sir. We're just checking out Mom's car."

"Glad to hear it," Mayor Witherspoon said. "Of course, if you do plan on hooking one, make sure you do it during our game. It might give me a fighting chance."

"Yes, sir," Blaine replied, giving a small salute.

"Afternoon, Mrs. Gallagher." The mayor nodded at Aunt Lenore. "How do you manage to look so lovely in this heat?"

"Now, now, Mr. Witherspoon." Aunt Lenore shook her index finger as if she were reprimanding him, but I could tell she loved every word.

"Hello, there, Cameron," the mayor greeted me.

"Hello, sir."

"You know, Blaine and I are playing a few holes tomorrow. Why don't you join us?"

I was on the verge of giving the mayor my standard refusal when Ashleigh leaned over her father's shoulder. "Go have some fun, Cam," she urged. "You've been working too hard."

Suddenly an idea sprang up. *That's it!* I told myself. *If I want Ashleigh, I should try and fit into her world. So what if I hate golf? If it helps me win Ashleigh, it's worth it.*

"Thanks, Mr. Witherspoon. I'd love to," I said.

Out of the corner of my eye I could see Blaine turn to gape at me.

"Fantastic!" Mayor Witherspoon exclaimed. "I'll meet you fellows here tomorrow at four."

Ashleigh waved once more before the mayor raised his tinted windows and slowly drove away.

As soon as the Lexus disappeared, Blaine got right in my face. "What do you think you're doing?" he demanded. "You can't come golf with us! Mom, tell him he can't."

Aunt Lenore patted his shoulder. "Blaine, honey, you were here. You heard the mayor invite him."

"But he's too busy to go, right?" Blaine asked his mom. "He's got to do a bunch of stuff for the pageant, right?"

"I agree with Ashleigh," Aunt Lenore said, smiling at me. "He deserves a break. Now, don't be a poor sport, Blaine, dear."

Blaine's jaw muscles quivered as he glared at me. "Don't think I don't know what you're doing!" he growled. "You're just jealous that I'm pals with the mayor, and you're trying to butt in to impress Ashleigh."

I shook my head. "No, Blaine. I—"

"Well, forget it," he hissed. "You don't have a chance."

I was so mad, I wanted to run him up the flagpole by his neatly ironed khakis. It took extreme control to prevent myself from losing it.

"And one more thing," Blaine said, shoving his index finger in my face. "If you end up embarrassing me and ruining my chances of making grand marshal, I'll kick your teeth in."

"Blaine!" Aunt Lenore gasped.

"You and how many marines?" I hissed.

But he just ignored us. After one final death stare he brushed past me, shoving my shoulder with his, and stalked toward the club. I could hardly believe it. I'd seen Blaine angry before, but never this upset.

"Don't pay too much attention to Blaine's little fit," Aunt Lenore said with a sigh. "He just really misses his father. I think that's why Mayor Witherspoon's approval means so much to him."

Her voice sounded far away, and she stared after Blaine with such a sad look, it made me forget my anger. I hadn't really thought about things that way. It probably was pretty tough for Blaine after Uncle Bert died. When Mom got hurt, I was totally scared and confused. And what Blaine went through must have been a hundred times worse.

"Maybe I shouldn't go," I offered. *After all,* I thought, *I can always golf with someone else if I want to show Ashleigh my more refined side.*

"No," Aunt Lenore said emphatically.

"But Blaine—"

"Blaine will be fine," she reassured. "It's only one game, after all. It's not like you're going to take up golfing as a pastime, right?"

Before I could answer, she was trotting off toward the club. Obviously she figured she already knew the answer.

Little did she know. From here on out, I was planning on doing lots of things I didn't normally do. I'd try anything to increase my chances with Ashleigh.

Note Passing in Calculus Class

Tracy,

Girl! Have I got some news! You'll never guess who Ashleigh Witherspoon has a thing for: Cameron Gallagher! I kid you not! I have no idea how that will go.

I mean, the guy might look just like a Calvin Klein ad, but he's also about as talkative. As far as I know, he *still* hasn't asked her out. Of course he probably has to rehearse it about two thousand times first.

Anyhow, stay tuned for further details! And *call me* if you hear/see anything, okay?

Tiffany

Nine

Gwenyth

"WHAT YEAR WAS the library built?" Larry read aloud. His knees bounced nervously as he sat cross-legged on the grass.

"1878," I replied.

"You want to make that your final answer?" he added, grinning.

I shot Larry a look that conveyed I was in no mood. He quickly passed the questions to Oscar, who cleared his voice and asked, "Where was the first schoolhouse located?"

"Trick question," I said, picking up a leaf and ripping it into tiny pieces. "It was where Kingstown High is now, on top of Mesa Hill."

I yawned gigantically and stretched out my arms. The guys had been quizzing me all day with the questions they'd compiled. They were so into it. Oscar had even typed them up and laser printed them. They gave the copy to me before school today, and I studied it during classes. Now here we were on the front lawn of the country club, trying to fit in one final cramming session before test time.

I was still not convinced I was doing the right thing by running for Queen. I *was* completely convinced of one thing, though: that Kingstown, Texas, made Mayberry look like a cultural Mecca.

"Who founded the town?" Bennett asked.

"Mr. Eli Kingston," I said, staring up at the sky. "He owned several acres of farmland and built most of the buildings downtown."

"Good answer!" Bennett said, handing the paper to Doyle.

"Let's stop, okay, Doyle?" I asked irritably. "I already know all this."

"Just a few more," he said. "What is the total current population of Kingstown?"

"Exactly 12,488," I cried impatiently. "Soon to be 12,481 if a certain seven individuals don't give me a break."

"Only two more short ones," Rom said. "Last spring the city council voted to build what?"

"A hockey rink."

"*Eecchhh!*" Rom made a noise like a buzzer going off. "Wrong. Try again."

"A Hard Rock Cafe."

"*Eecchhh!*" Rom went again.

"Rom!" Larry screeched. "If you do that

again, I'll disintegrate you down to your basic chemical elements!"

"Come on, Gwen," Haskell pleaded. "Just give us the right answer. We're almost done."

"A new city hall," I mumbled, sitting back up and picking the dead grass out of my hair.

"And where will it be located?" Terry asked.

"Guys, this is useless!" I snapped, startling Terry into dropping the paper. "What if none of the questions on the test come close to these? What if we're just wasting our time?"

"Gwen, Gwen, Gwen." Doyle clasped his hands and assumed an authoritative tone of voice. "Kingstown history isn't all that long or eventful. There are very good odds that this material will be on the test."

I shut my eyes and took a deep breath. "I'm sorry. I guess I'm just nervous. You guys worked so hard researching all this, and I'll feel terrible if I let you down."

"You won't, Gwen," Doyle said.

The other guys voiced their agreements.

I smiled. It actually was really nice of them to have so much faith in me. And I knew that even if I totally blew the test and embarrassed myself, I'd still have them to hang around with. After Bree and her gang turning on me, not to mention all the confusion with Tony's slick moves, I realized how hard it was to find good, sincere friends.

"I think it's time for me to go in," I said, looking at my watch. Terry offered me the study sheet, but I refused it. "It won't do me any good now," I explained. "Either I know this stuff or I don't."

"You're going to pass it, no problem," Doyle declared. "I know it."

The gang shouted words of encouragement as I headed into the club. Once inside, I followed the bright pink poster-board arrows reading Fall Festival Pageant until I reached a conference room. I walked in and saw the other contestants sitting at tables that were neatly spaced apart throughout the room. They were all scanning index cards or marked-up pieces of paper. All except Bree. She sat calmly near the front, her hands neatly clasped on the tabletop.

As soon as she saw me she smiled, lifted up a copy of *A Brief History of Kingstown,* and placed it ceremoniously in front of her. I knew immediately what she was telling me. It couldn't have been coincidence that all available copies of the book disappeared from the town.

I lifted my chin and walked past her, taking a seat in the back of the room. Two minutes later the door opened and the lady from the assembly bustled in, holding a stack of papers.

"Please put away all study materials, young ladies," she announced. "I will now give each of you a copy of the test. Take as long as you need to answer the questions, but you may not start until everyone is ready."

She wove around the tables and placed a paper facedown in front of each girl with a dramatic, sweeping gesture. Then she walked back to the front of the room, waited a few seconds as if to purposefully create suspense, and proclaimed, "You may now begin."

The air filled with the sounds of rippling paper and the scratching of pencils. I hesitated. *You can do this*, I told myself. *Just give it your best shot.*

I flipped the paper and read the first question. *What is the current population of Kingstown?* I exhaled in relief and scrawled out the answer. At least the guys predicted that one.

Next question: *Who founded Kingstown?* Score two for the guys. Maybe I wouldn't do too badly after all.

Question three: *Where was the first schoolhouse located?* Hmmm. It struck me as odd that they would see that one coming. How lucky could I get?

I quickly glanced over the rest of the test questions to see if I could predict my score. Then it hit me. I knew all of them. These were the same questions the guys printed out for me! They were in a different order, but otherwise they exactly matched the ones on my study sheet!

The odds of that happening seemed way too impossible to calculate—even for Doyle and the gang.

Cameron

That *was one major mistake,* I told myself as I headed into the club's air-conditioned interior, right behind Blaine and Mayor Witherspoon. *I should have never agreed to this stupid golf game.*

What a farce it was. First, Blaine kept kissing up to the mayor the entire time, complimenting him on his shots and making one lame joke after the other. I didn't speak unless spoken to—which Blaine only did if he was asking me to fetch his nine iron. The mayor at least tried to make small talk. He asked me all about school and my job and my mom's injury. I knew he was just being polite, but it only made me uncomfortable. I mean, what if he'd been sizing me up?

At least my game didn't suck too bad. I beat the mayor by one stroke, and Blaine beat me by four.

"You kids sure know how to embarrass an old geezer," the mayor said, laughing.

Blaine kept right on his heels. "No way!" he said. "Your form is really coming along."

"Cameron! You still with us?" The mayor stopped in his tracks and turned to face me. "Come have a soda. My treat."

Actually, I could have used a drink. Blaine managed to down all but one of the plastic bottles of water we kept in the cooler. I hated the thought of stretching the experience out even further, but I was really hot and thirsty. Plus I didn't want to appear ungrateful to the mayor.

"Thanks," I said, falling into step behind him. Blaine shot me a dirty look, making a total of 137 for the afternoon.

We sat at a table near the bar, and a waiter brought us over some iced teas.

"Thanks for humoring an old guy, boys,"

Mayor Witherspoon said after taking a long swig.

"You're not old, Mr. Witherspoon." Blaine shook his head. "In fact, it seems impossible for you to have a seventeen-year-old daughter."

The mayor looked down at the tabletop and smiled to himself. "Ashleigh is what keeps me young. She's a real godsend." He reached over and clapped me on the back. "Isn't that right, Cameron?"

I nodded in a circular motion like one of those dopey toy Chihuahuas. "Yes, sir. She's . . . incredible," I said without thinking.

Immediately I regretted it. The mayor laughed heartily, and Blaine joined right in. I shrank down to the size of a zit.

"I think I need to go," I said, pushing back my chair.

"No! Not yet," the mayor said, his chuckles subsiding. "Don't tell me Lenore's got you fixing more cars?"

"No, sir. But I have other stuff to do."

"You know, that reminds me." The mayor rubbed his chin with one hand and plopped the other one down on my shoulder. "Lenore's been telling me what a great job you did on her car. There's this problem I've been having with the 400. Since your dad's out of town, could you take a look sometime?"

"Uh . . . s-sure," I stammered.

"That's great, just great," Mayor Witherspoon said, whacking me on my back. "It must be nice to understand those dang cars. Boy, I tell you, my Lexus made me so mad the other day, I seriously

111

considered driving it into Lake Mathis."

"Yeah, I know," Blaine jumped in. "My car does this thing where it idles real rough when I start it."

"Really?" The mayor leaned toward Blaine's side of the table. "I had a Benz that did that same thing."

The two of them chatted away about overheating radiators and slipping transmissions. Normally this would have been a discussion I could dive right into, but not this time. It was glaringly apparent that I didn't belong—in the conversation, the golf game, the club, or any part of their big-bank-account world. They got to drive the fancy cars. I could only fix them.

And that life was what Ashleigh was used to. I thought I could fake it, but I couldn't. No matter how hard I tried.

"Excuse me, but I really should get going," I said, standing. "Thanks for the game. And the drink."

"Do you have to?" the mayor asked, looking at his Rolex.

"I'm afraid so. I promised Aunt Lenore I'd clear the conference room after the queen contestants finished their tests."

"Well, okay, then." Mayor Witherspoon grabbed my hand and shook it firmly. "Good game, sport."

"Likewise. I'll see you around," I said, nodding. Then as politely as I could, I added, "See you, Blaine."

I crossed the dining area and entered the main hallway, quickly marching past the doors to the terrace. There was no way I could face Ashleigh. Not after that humiliation. Talking with her would only make it worse.

The thing was, she'd been so cool toward me lately. I was halfway certain that if I asked her out, she'd say yes. But this wasn't just any girl or any old date to the movies. This was Ashleigh. If we went out together, I'd completely lose my soul to her. Which meant it would really mess me up if things didn't work out.

And now I had to face the fact that things would never, *ever* happen between us.

I slumped down in a nearby lounge chair and shut my eyes. I felt totally sick and disoriented. It made me wonder if this was what my mom experienced during her accident: a strange falling sensation followed by a deadening ache. It could have been heatstroke from all that golfing without fluids, but something told me it wasn't.

For years I had cultivated this hope that I would one day end up with Ashleigh. It had always been there, like some vital part of me—just as crucial at keeping me going as my heart and lungs. That was why it hurt so bad to realize I had no chance with her. It literally felt like a piece of me was dying.

Marissa

I paced in front of our living-room window, biting my nails, while Dad sat in the kitchen, reading *Newsweek*. He was seemingly calm, but I knew better.

Fry was coming over. We needed to paint the backdrop, and the only way Dad would agree to it was if we worked here—under his supervision. Just the thought of them being throwing distance away from each other made me jittery. I wondered if referees felt this way before a Mike Tyson fight.

A rap sounded at the door, making me jump. I raced over and opened it wide.

Fry stood on the porch, holding a large, cardboard box full of supplies. "Hey," he said.

"Hi!" I said, a little too loudly. "Come on in. We can go through the side door to the garage."

I yanked Fry inside and steered him through the living room and kitchen. I was just about to open the door to the garage when Dad stood up noisily from the table.

"Marissa," he said gruffly.

I gulped. "Yeah?"

"Keep the door unlocked." He stared at Fry threateningly.

"Oo-kay," I sang, as if nothing was wrong.

Fry and I went into the garage, and I shut the door behind me, taking care not to close it too fast and risk appearing eager or too slow and have it seem like I was afraid.

"Your dad's pretty stressed about me being here, huh?" Fry asked, nodding back toward the kitchen.

I wasn't sure what to say. I didn't want him to feel bad, but I couldn't exactly deny it either. "He's just superprotective," I said with a shrug. "You know dads."

"Nice space here," he said, setting his box down on the floor. "This where you usually work?"

I shook my head. "Nah. I do my own stuff in Ms. Crowley's room during advisory. The equipment's better, and it's quieter. Also, I work better when I'm by myself."

Fry looked at me pointedly, and I realized what I'd just said.

"I mean," I added, "I work better when I'm away from home."

"It's okay. I know I sort of muscled in on your turf."

His comment caught me off guard. I always figured Fry had no clue that he was butting into my private time in the art room. The more I thought about it, though, the more I realized he was there for the same reasons I was. It wasn't like he fit in anyplace else. In fact, he probably hated school as much as I did—maybe even more.

"So here's what I think should happen today," Fry said, doing a perfect imitation of Ms. Crowley's New Agey voice. He shut his eyes and gestured into the air. "I see you marking out the patterns onto the plywood. And I see me cutting them with the circular saw. Two people, working side by side in perfect harmony."

In spite of my anxiety I couldn't help but laugh out loud. He was so dead-on.

Suddenly Dad threw open the door and leaned inside. "What's all that noise?" he demanded.

"Nothing, Dad," I said. "We're just joking around."

He frowned at us for a few seconds before

disappearing back into the kitchen. After that, the mood became stiff again.

I looked at Fry and wrinkled my nose apologetically. "Sorry," I murmured.

"It's okay," he said, lifting his shoulders. "I'm used to it."

We got right to work. While I traced our designs onto the plywood, Fry cut them out with the power saw. When we finished, we spaced the plywood patterns on top of the tarpaulin I'd set out earlier and knelt down to paint.

With the power saw off, it was totally silent. You'd think it would be awkward, but it wasn't. I felt like I did when I'd work in Ms. Crowley's room, just concentrating on the work and nothing else. In fact, *concentrating* wasn't the right word since it implies effort. When I got into this mode, it was like I *became* the work. My mind cleared, and my body simply knew what to do. I'd never been able to do that alongside someone else before.

We opened the garage doors, and as we finished painting each piece of backdrop, Fry would drag it out to dry in the sun. Eventually we got down to painting the last two cutouts.

"Oops," Fry said, holding up his paint can. "I just ran out of black."

"That's okay. I have more here somewhere." I stood and scanned the shelves along the wall behind him. Sure enough, there sat a half gallon of black. I walked up next to Fry, stepped onto a small crate, and stretched my right arm way up to reach the can. For some reason, I still had my paintbrush in my left hand (it sort of became part of your body when you were an artist), and as it dangled over Fry, blue paint started to drip on him.

"Hey!" he exclaimed.

"Oh, sorry!" I said, glancing down. As soon as I saw him, I started laughing. The paint had fallen onto his head and ran down the middle of his forehead and nose.

Fry flicked his brush at me, splattering black across my calf. "Oops. Sorry," he said, smirking.

I waved my brush his direction, showering more blue paint on his face. "My mistake," I said, grinning.

"Oh, no *prob*-lem!" He lunged forward and whisked his paintbrush over my stomach, making a long, black slash mark on my shirt.

Then it was war. I hopped off the box, and we laughed and shouted and charged back and forth at each other in a paint-flinging sword fight.

Soon all the paint had come off Fry's brush. When he realized he was out of ammunition, he shielded his face with his arms and started backing up. "No fair!" he said, chuckling. "You have the big brush. I had the little one for outlining."

"Yep. I'm bigger and badder!" I cried victoriously.

"Oh yeah?" Fry dove for my brush and ended up knocking me over. Luckily we both tumbled onto the pile of old blankets we'd been using as drop cloths.

I lay on my back, trying to keep hold of the

paintbrush as I laughed hysterically. Meanwhile Fry knelt over me, also laughing as he tried to wrench the brush out of my hands. But every time he yanked up on it, the bristles would sweep across his face. Soon his features were completely smeared with watery blue paint.

"Someone help!" I hooted. "I'm being attacked by a Teletubby!"

All of a sudden the kitchen door banged open. "Get off of her *now!*" my dad's voice thundered.

Fry and I leaped apart, and the large paintbrush skittered across the floor.

Purple veins stood out on his forehead as Dad glared at Fry. "Go inside, Marissa," he growled without looking at me.

"Dad, it's okay. We were just kidding around," I tried to explain.

"Go inside now!" he hissed. He turned his eyes on me, and I could see his entire body was shaking. Suddenly I was afraid—not necessarily for me or Fry, but for my dad's health.

I quickly dashed through the open kitchen door but stopped just on the other side to listen.

"If I ever see you set one foot onto my property," Dad snarled, "I will call the police!"

"Look, sir. You've got it all wrong," I could hear Fry say. It amazed me how calm and respectful he sounded.

"Don't you dare talk to me! Get out of my house!"

"I know what you must be thinking," Fry tried again, "but it was just a—"

"Now!" Dad's voice was shaky and high-pitched. I was so scared that any minute now he'd have another heart attack. All because of me.

"Just leave, Fry," I cried, leaning through the doorway. "Get out of here!"

Fry looked at me, completely stunned. Then he quickly glanced away.

Dad continued to stare menacingly at Fry until he'd gathered his stuff into his box, hoisted it, and trudged down our concrete driveway toward his house. As soon as Fry was out of sight, Dad turned toward me.

"Marissa, you are never to talk to that boy again," he said hoarsely. "Do you hear?" His fists had unclenched, and his normal color was back. Now he just looked weary.

"Dad! You don't understand," I whined. "He didn't do anything wrong."

"Don't argue with me!" Dad barked.

"Fine," I snapped. I quickly spun around and re-treated into the house. There was no talking to Dad when he got this way. And I didn't want to risk him losing it again either.

As soon as I reached my room, I locked the door and threw myself onto my bed. I felt utterly lousy. There were so many bad feelings inside me, I could hardly count them. I was scared for Dad. I was angry he wouldn't listen to me. I was worried he'd make me quit art.

And I was really, *really* confused about Fry.

*   *   *

FROM THE DESK OF LENORE GALLAGHER

Fall Festival Queen Contestant Test Scores

Marcy Whitfield: 73
Tracy Reed: 80
Sherry Wynn: 88
Tisha Adams: 65
Linda Loftin: 92
Denise Russo: 58
Bree Hampton: 95
Gwenyth Darby: 100

Ten

Gwenyth

"HELLO?"

"Hi, Doyle? It's Gwen."

There was a slight pause. "Oh, hey," he said, ultracasual. "How did it go?"

"Fine. Great, in fact." I sat down on my bed and shifted the phone to the other ear.

"Really?" I could almost hear him squirm. "That's good. So . . . it wasn't hard?"

"Not at all. Especially when you consider that *I'd been studying the exact same test all day!*"

"Wh-What are you talking about?" Doyle might have been a genius, but he was no actor.

"Don't treat me like I'm stupid, Doyle. Don't tell me it was coincidence or luck or that great Kingstown minds think alike. I know you guys cheated!"

There was an audible sigh from the other end. "Okay, yeah. I knew you'd figure it out."

"Duh! You guys didn't even change the wording of the questions! How could I not figure it out?"

"Yeah," Doyle mumbled. "I told them we should change it up more."

"God, I felt so weird. As soon as I realized what you guys did, it occurred to me that I should tell Mrs. Gallagher."

I could hear him suck in his breath. "Did you?" he asked solemnly.

"No, of course not. I would never do that." I brought my voice down to a normal level. "But I want to know why. Why'd you guys cheat? Did you think I wasn't smart enough to pass otherwise?"

"No! That's not it! We just panicked. I mean, we got you into this, but we never figured all the books would be gone, and we didn't know how to help you study otherwise, so then Oscar suggested we do it, and he knew how, so we just let him."

"Whoa. Slow down." I'd never heard Doyle spaz out before. He sounded so *guilty*. "What did Oscar do, Doyle? You guys didn't break into the club, did you?"

Doyle blew out his breath, making the phone sound all staticky. "Worse," he said finally. "Breaking and entering is a class-B misdemeanor. But hacking into someone's computer . . ."

"You didn't!"

"You know, you'd think they would make it harder," Doyle mused. "But these online neighborhood networks are a cinch to crack. Oscar always said he knew how, but he never tried it. When we told him to go ahead, it was almost like a dare. We didn't think he really could."

"Oh my God!"

"Yeah. No kidding. I'm canceling my membership tomorrow."

"But Doyle! You guys actually broke the law! You're felons."

"Jeez, Gwen, it's not like we put out the Melissa virus or interrupted e-commerce for twelve hours," Doyle retorted. "All we did was help you out."

I shook my head. "I don't feel right about this."

"Let me remind you of something," he said. The old Doyle know-it-all voice was back in full strength. "Do you think all those copies of the Kingstown history just *happened* to get checked out and bought up? I don't buy it. I'm telling you, Bree Hampton was doing some foul play of her own."

I didn't say anything. I remembered Bree flaunting her copy at me before the test and realized he had a point. That girl would obviously stoop pretty low to win the dumb contest. Why should she be the only one getting away with it?

"Come on, Gwen," Doyle pleaded. "You're not going to back out on moral grounds now, are you?"

Again I thought about Bree's smug face, and a lust for revenge boiled up inside me. If I quit now, that girl would think I was intimidated by her. No way would I let her get that satisfaction.

"Don't worry. I'm still in," I said.

"Great!"

"But you've got to promise me you guys won't do anything else illegal," I added.

"We won't," Doyle said reassuringly. "Eagle Scout's honor."

Marissa

The large, red numbers on my alarm clock read 1:37. I rolled over onto my left side and folded my pillow around my head, trying to muffle my thoughts.

For two hours I'd tossed and turned while the evening's events replayed in my mind like a bad movie. If only I'd never told my dad about having to work with Fry. If only I'd figured out a way to paint the backdrop somewhere else. If only I'd kept things quiet so Dad wouldn't have gotten worried.

I reached down to scratch a spot of paint on my shin and smiled. It hadn't been all bad. Working with Fry had been a blast before Dad barged in. I hadn't had that much fun in a long time.

I quickly sat up and threw my quilt off me. Sleep was totally beyond my powers tonight. Might as well get up and draw. At least I'd be using the time productively.

The cool air from the window hit me as I climbed out of bed and headed for my desk. Just as I was about to switch on my desk lamp, I heard the distinct *chung* sound of something hitting metal, followed by a person muttering irritably. I tiptoed to the window and listened.

"Jeez, not again," came a guy's voice.

That's when I noticed a light shining off the top of the garage across the street—Fry's garage. Someone was sitting on the roof with a lantern or flashlight. I studied the person's outline in detail: long legs, slumped shoulders, wild mop of hair. It was Fry. Obviously he couldn't sleep either. But what was he doing?

Beside him I could see the unmistakable outline of a bottle. Oh no. Surely he wasn't stupid enough to drink alcohol in clear view of the neighbors? Or at such a dangerous height?

Then again, Fry probably didn't care.

I decided to go over and see him. I had wanted to apologize to him, and now here was my chance.

I pulled on a pair of shorts under my big University of Texas sleep shirt and slowly pushed my window open wider. Then I carefully undid the bottom two latches of the screen, slipped outside, and made my way across our front lawn. As soon as I was certain the coast was clear, I scurried across the road to Fry's house.

Fry hadn't noticed me. I stood next to his motorcycle and craned my head upward. He sat facing the downward slope of the roof, his knees bent at an angle to provide a work surface on his lap. I could see his arms moving and hear the scraping sound of a pencil against paper.

"Drawing something?" I called out.

Fry gave a slight yelp of surprise. His pencil flew out of his hand and rolled down the roof's incline, landing in the gutter with a loud *chung*. "Damn! Not again," he exclaimed. Then he peered over the edge at me. "What are you doing here?"

I shrugged and nervously shifted my weight on my bare feet. "Nothing," I replied.

"Couldn't sleep?" he asked.

I shook my head.

Fry smiled crookedly, the lantern halfway illuminating his face. "There's a ladder on the other side," he said, jerking a thumb behind him. "Come on up."

In the cool night air with every little noise echoing in the darkness, I suddenly felt really self-conscious. What was I doing, getting on the roof in the middle of the night with a clearly strange and possibly drunk guy? If Dad found out, he'd probably kill me and Fry, then suffer a massive coronary. On the other hand, I was experiencing a definite thrill at being out here—as if I'd just escaped from prison.

I padded around to the wooden ladder leaning against the back of the garage and slowly climbed onto the roof. Soon there was nothing around me but stars. I took a few wobbly steps over to Fry and sat down.

"Here," he said, handing me a cold, brown glass bottle.

"Oh, uh . . ." I hesitated, wondering how I could refuse his drink without insulting him. As I awkwardly turned it around in my hands, the label caught my eye: Root beer. I almost laughed out loud. "Thanks," I said, twisting off the cap.

"Sure," Fry replied with a nod.

"So, what are you doing out here?" I asked.

"I'm *trying* to write a letter," he explained, holding up a spiral notebook. "Only I keep losing my pencils. I had a whole pack of five, and now three have already rolled away from me."

"Yeah. Sorry about that," I said, chuckling. "You better get those out of your gutter before the next big thunderstorm."

Fry lifted an eyebrow at me. "Yes, ma'am," he drawled in a terrible Texas accent.

I ignored it. "Who are you writing to?"

"My art teacher at Reese," he said, staring out at the inky black horizon.

"Oh," I replied. "What are you writing about?"

Fry shot me a baffled expression. "Interesting question," he said. "Here's another one: What are *you* doing here?"

"Nothing," I mumbled, slowly ripping the label off my bottle of root beer. "I just . . . wanted to apologize for . . . you know. For the way my dad freaked out and all."

He set down his notebook and stretched his legs out in front of him. "No big deal," he said.

"Really?" I asked, squinting at him. "Don't you get tired of people assuming you're some insane drug addict?"

Fry scowled up at the sky. "I didn't used to. That is," he added, looking right at me, "until recently."

I stared back at him, a tingly warmth jetting up from inside me. At the same time a strong gust of wind blew between us, rippling our shirts and lifting the hair away from our faces. Without the filter of his scraggly bangs, Fry's big, gray eyes seemed to smolder, as if giving off their own light.

A woozy, unbalanced feeling suddenly came over me. Was it the root beer? Lack of sleep? The steep incline of the roof?

Or was I actually falling for Fry Darby?

Cameron

The night after the golf game was awful. I couldn't sleep no matter what. My body was all hot and achy, as if I were the victim of some exotic flu, and I couldn't stop thinking about Ashleigh.

Maybe that was the real reason I ached.

Finally—at some painfully late hour—I fell into a tense sleep and was confronted by the most amazing dream I'd ever had in my life. It was so realistic, it was spooky.

I was sitting on Aunt Lenore's porch swing, talking with my uncle Bert, just like we always used to do. I could smell the nearby cedar trees and feel the warm breeze across my face. I could even hear the high-pitched squeak of the swing's chains. Uncle Bert sat on the steps, looking at me. The entire time I knew him, he always seemed to be wearing one of two expressions: either an all-out, face-cracking, denture-showing grin or a quiet smile. This time he had on the latter.

"Don't be so down on yourself, Cam," Uncle Bert said in his cheerful drawl.

"I can't help it, Uncle Bert," I said, dragging my feet over the porch floor as I swung back and forth. "I've been fooling myself for so long, it's sort of hard to face reality."

Uncle Bert's eyebrows knitted together. "Fooling yourself about what?"

"Thinking I had a chance with Ashleigh," I mumbled. "Thinking I could deserve her if I just tried hard enough."

"What's wrong with all that thinking? Doesn't sound foolish to me."

I sighed and looked out at the cedars. "But Blaine's right. I'm not in her league. I can't even pretend to be."

"Don't take what Blaine says too seriously." Uncle Bert shook his head. "He's just jealous of you."

"Yeah, right." I snorted.

"It's true." Uncle Bert took a cigarette out of his shirt pocket and stuck it in between his lips. Then he cupped a hand around it as if it were incredibly fragile and lit it with a match. The scent of burning Marlboro immediately drowned out the spice of cedar. This was why we always talked on the porch. Aunt Lenore was afraid of the smell getting into her fancy furniture.

"Why would he be jealous of me?" I asked.

"You're good at something," he replied, tapping his ashes onto the ground below. "You've always been mechanically minded, like your dad. And someday you'll be a great engineer. Blaine wants to be good at golf the way you are at fixing things. But he's not. Nope, Blaine's like his mama. Good at talking and spending money."

I stopped swinging and rested my elbows on my knees. "You know, I always wished I could talk to people the way Blaine does. He can talk to anyone anytime. Not me, though. I'm too shy. Especially with girls."

Uncle Bert flashed me his other, wider smile. "Yep. The Gallagher men aren't known for being able to chat folks up. Your dad and I were that way growing up too. I couldn't approach a girl if she had me on a leash!" He threw back his head and laughed.

"But what about you and Aunt Lenore?" I asked when he stopped chuckling. "How'd you guys get together?"

His grin turned wistful. "It was fate," he replied. "I was so crazy about her. I admired her confidence and the easy way she had with people. Man, that woman could talk! I guess it's true what they say about opposites attracting. But you know, I would have never gotten her if I hadn't gotten up the gumption to ask her out. . . ."

Uncle Bert's last few words echoed through my head as the sights and smells of the porch faded away. I blinked open my eyes and found myself once again in Aunt Lenore's flowery guest room. I sat up, disoriented. It took a few moments for me to realize that it had only been a dream. Uncle Bert was still gone. Nothing had changed.

But one thing *had* changed. Real or not, Uncle Bert's words had filled me with willpower: *I would have never gotten her if I hadn't gotten up the gumption to ask her out. . . .*

The only thing foolish about my feelings for Ashleigh was that I was thinking about giving up. I should at least ask her out, if only once. After all, we Gallagher men might not be big talkers—but we certainly weren't fools.

Dear Ron,

Man, I almost wrote, Dear Mr. Croft. A few months in this place and I'm already conditioned against calling teachers by their first names.

Life is hell here. It's certainly hot enough, and there are quite a few ranchers with pitchforks. Of course, they all think I'm one of the crazed criminals they see on NYPD Blue. For all they know, I'm here to rob them, sell drugs, and reset all their radio dials from country to hard rock.

I am taking your advice and doing my art. I signed up for their advanced class and found out that the teacher here is actually pretty cool. And there's this other student in the class who's also cool. Her name is Marissa, and she's a really good sketch artist. She's also beautiful. Great bone structure and the most amazing long, dark, wavy hair. I want so badly to sculpt her.

I know, I know. You're saying, "Oh no. Brian's in love? Again?" But it's different this time. There's just something about this girl. Since we moved here, I've purposefully tried to be the most monstrous jerk ever, just to keep everyone away. But Marissa actually saw through it. In fact, she hates it here too. Besides my sister and new art teacher, she's the only one who isn't a total phony.

Anyway, you don't have to freak out that I might do something stupid. I'm not running away—at least, not soon. But if you're still worried, feel free to send lots and lots of cash.

Your ex-student (and best ever),

Brian Darby

Eleven

Gwenyth

THE DAY BEFORE the pageant, Mrs. Gallagher worked us so hard, I almost forgot to feel bad about cheating. She made us run through the entire pageant over and over. Then, when she was sure we had it down, she let us take turns doing our talent numbers onstage. I went last.

Once I'd finished practicing, it was already late, and I still had to drop off my evening gown at the town's dry cleaner's for some last-minute alterations. I quickly changed shoes, grabbed my gym bag, threw my dress over my shoulder, and headed out to the parking lot. But as I approached my car, something didn't look right. The front end seemed all lopsided. Finally I got close enough to see the problem: The front right tire was completely flat.

"Oh no!" I shouted, dropping my gym bag.

I slowly circled my car like some overgrown buzzard in a pink leotard, assessing the situation. I was royally out of luck. No spare, no possibility of driving it, and only ten minutes before the dry cleaner's closed. Even if I held my dress over my head and started running, there was no way I could make it there in time.

"Hey! Need some help?" someone called out.

I turned and saw a blue Blazer rolling up beside me. The driver's-side window was down, and Tony Etheridge sat behind the wheel, grinning. He looked like some sort of divine vision. All that was missing was the telltale ray of sunlight streaming through the clouds.

"I've got a flat," I said.

"I can see that," he replied. "Got a spare?"

"No."

"Can I give you a lift?" His grin spread across his face, lighting up his eyes and pressing in his dimples. This was the image I'd been trying like mad to erase since I'd run into him at the library. I'd thought I was finally over this ridiculous crush. I really did. But now here he was in front of me, and my heart was leaping inside me like a puppy overjoyed to see its master.

"I . . . don't . . . think . . . so," I forced myself to say, rather unconvincingly.

Tony looked perplexed. "Um . . . you know, it's not like you have a lot of options."

"I can walk," I said, picking up my gym bag and heading out of the parking lot. The Blazer continued to roll along beside me.

"I know you're not from these parts," Tony said, "but down here we help people out when they need it. It's called being neighborly."

I didn't say anything. *Don't listen to him,* I told myself. *Remember what the guys said.*

"Come on, Gwen. Please?"

The sound of him saying my name caused all sorts of fluttering sensations inside me. I wished he would either drive off or shut up. I considered covering my ears and going, "La, la, la!" as loud as I could, only my hands were full.

"You know, it's getting dark. And they still haven't caught the guy who's bashing in the mailboxes. I really think you should just accept the ride," Tony added, his voice all serious.

I came to a stop. My arms were starting to ache, and it was getting hard to see the road. Tony had a point about it getting dark.

"Okay," I said with a sigh. "But would you mind stopping by the dry cleaner's first?"

Tony's high-voltage grin reappeared. "No problem!" he said.

I checked for traffic, crossed the street, and ran around to his passenger door. As I climbed in, the faint scent of his cologne emanated from the plush interior.

"I bet you're excited about the pageant," he said, drumming his hands on the steering wheel. "After all, you've got the best chance at winning."

"Yeah, right," I said, staring down at my lap.

"No, seriously," he replied. "You could teach all those girls a thing or two. That's why I nominated you."

I turned and gaped at him. *He* turned in the mysterious tenth nomination form? It had been him all along? Sitting in the twilight, breathing in Tony's musky aftershave, I had the distinct feeling I'd entered another plane of existence.

"Here's the cleaner's," Tony announced, pulling the car up to the entrance.

My mind was so jumbled with questions, it was almost difficult for me to move. Somehow, though, I managed to go inside and hand my dress to the girl behind the counter. By the time I reached the Blazer again, my brain had cleared.

"Okay," I said, slamming the car door. "Who put you up to it? Doyle? Bennett? Rom?"

Tony looked baffled. "No one," he said. "It was my idea."

"But why?" I asked.

He grinned sort of sheepishly. "Because someone like you deserves it."

I shook my head. "I don't understand. What do you mean, 'someone like me'?"

"Someone cool. Someone . . . real. For years it's always gone to the most popular senior girl in school, like it's some unwritten law. I know Bree thinks it's her God-given right, but I'm sick of the way she treats people. The girl's on a major power trip."

Again I could feel my jaw unhinge. "You . . . you think Bree's on a power trip," I repeated, trying to make sense of it all. Only Tony took it as a question.

"Yeah. Don't you?" he asked.

"Well, yeah. But . . ." I still couldn't believe he

was saying this. The very idea was bouncing in my mind like a rubber ball. "But I thought you two were, sort of, together."

Tony made a face. "What gave you that idea?"

"Because you're always walking to class with her."

"No. *She's* always walking to class with *me*," he said, chuckling. "And lately she's really been hinting around about me asking her to the Fall Festival dance. But there's someone else I want to ask. Only . . . she never sticks around long enough to hear me out."

I slowly moved my eyeballs and then the rest of my face toward him. He was staring at me expectantly. His expression was all tight and nervous looking, but it only made him more adorable.

"Gwen?" he said. "Will you go to the dance with me?"

Oh no! Oh, jeez! What do I do now? I didn't trust myself to think clearly on this one. I wanted so badly to say yes. But the rest of me kept remembering what the guys had said, about Tony making me his next victim. Who should I believe? Him? Or the guys who'd been standing by me the way no one else had since I moved here?

"I . . . don't know," I said, glancing down at the car's floorboards. "I mean, I've got this pageant thing. And I don't really know you that well. And I'm just not sure about anyone in this place. Things are so different. I'm not even sure I fit in. *Aaugh!*" I grunted, grabbing my forehead to try and stop my rambling. "I wish I'd never moved here!"

He was quiet for a moment, then looked at me.

"Hey, listen. Forget about going out together. You've got a lot on your mind. But promise me you'll look for me after you're crowned queen and maybe save me a dance?"

My cheeks gradually lifted, pulling my lips apart in a smile. "Sure," I replied. I turned to look at him, and right at that moment the dry cleaner's sign snapped off, leaving us in near total darkness.

"Um . . . I guess I better drive you home," he said softly.

"Yeah. I guess so," I replied.

We drove along the quiet roads without talking. I was still a mess of confusion. Yet in the middle of it all, for the first time since I moved here, I could feel a sense of hope.

Marissa

I parked my dad's gargantuan green Suburban in front of the country club and opened the rear door. Inside, the painted pieces of the backdrop lay in neat little stacks.

"Pssst!" came a noise from behind.

I turned and saw Fry's sheepdog hairdo appear around a brick column.

"Are you alone?" Fry whispered loudly.

"Yes," I replied. "I swore to my dad that the people at the club would help me unload these. And thankfully my mom wouldn't let him come and help out because of his condition. We're in the clear."

"Whew! That's good," he exclaimed, the rest of him emerging.

I was glad to see him. And not just because I'd be getting some help with all the work. After hanging out with him the other night, I felt like we'd bonded somehow. Like two buddies—or possibly even closer. In some strange, unspoken way I felt like Fry knew me better than anyone. It was weird to think how uncomfortable I used to be around him.

After several trips we managed to carry most of the cutouts into the ballroom. Soon all that remained was the small stuff.

"Cool," I said as we dumped the last heavy load onto the stage. "Just one more run and we'll have it all."

"I'll get it," Fry said.

I shook my head. "No. I'll come. It isn't much."

Fry smiled. "Exactly. That's why I'll do it myself. Besides"—he gently nudged me under the chin with his hand—"you look tired. I don't want you to overdo it."

Normally I would have reamed him for making a sexist comment. But I didn't. And perhaps normally he would have made that remark with a smirk. But he didn't. Instead he let his fingers linger on my face. His big, gray eyes seemed to rummage through me as if searching for an answer. Only I wasn't sure what the question was. I was only aware of the softness of his gaze and the softness of his touch.

"Be back in a sec," Fry murmured before heading out the side door.

I stood watching him, waiting for the fluttery feelings inside me to subside.

"What the hell are you doing?" Blaine Gallagher's voice echoed across the ballroom, startling me. My flutters vanished completely, replaced by sinking dread.

"What are you talking about?" I replied, trying to sound as snide as possible.

Blaine stepped forward into the light cast from the stage. "Don't give me that," he said, his upper lip curled in disdain. "I saw you getting all chummy with that burnout."

My heartbeat revved up to panic mode. I knew I had real feelings for Fry—there was no question about it now—but I wasn't ready to tell the world yet. It was too new, too strange, and too special. Besides, my dad did the club's books for Blaine's mom. What if Blaine told her about me and Fry and she told Dad?

"Look, I don't know what you think you saw, but you're freaking," I said calmly.

"You're the one that's freaking," Blaine retorted. "What gives, Marissa? First you go all goth, then you act like you're too good to hang with us, and now you hook up with some druggie? Why would you want him when you know you can have Will?"

All I could do was glower at him. I wanted so badly to tell him off—to say how Fry was a million times better than Will Benson and that my social life was none of his business. But there was just no explaining things to a thumb-head jock like Blaine. It would only make him more determined. Somehow I had to get him to back off before he jeopardized both my relationship with my dad and whatever it was starting between me and Fry.

"I told you last time. I'm only spending time with Fry because I have to," I said. "Don't go spreading around lies about me. If my dad hears about me being nice to Fry, he'll lose it."

Blaine's face turned smug again. I could hear the "what's in it for me?" coming my way.

"I'm serious, Blaine," I added. "My dad despises Fry. He thinks he's a criminal. In fact, he's convinced Fry's behind all the mailbox smashings."

"Really?" Blaine perked up even more. "Interesting."

"So can I count on you to keep your big mouth shut? *Please?*" I asked, all the while realizing how hopeless it was to appeal to Blaine Gallagher's conscience.

Blaine stared up at the ceiling for a moment, a sly grin creeping across the lower half of his face. Finally he held up one hand and placed the other over his heart. "I promise," he said without a hint of sarcasm. "Your father won't hear about any of this from me."

I squinted at him. "You're serious?"

"Positive," he said. Then he puffed up his chest and added in a self-important tone, "Now, if you'll excuse me, I need to go see the mayor."

Big whoop, I thought as I watched him exit the ballroom.

I really, *really* hoped I could trust Blaine. I hated having to lie and beg, but at least I seemed to throw him off. Lately I had far too many people scrutinizing my life: my dad, Will, Blaine. All I wanted was to figure out what was going on between me and Fry, without anyone else's interference.

I looked over at our heap of backdrop sections. Just another hour of work and our project would be over. I would never have to spend another second with Fry. Bizarre how only a few days ago I thought this moment would never come. Now I didn't want it to.

But project or not, I knew I still had to see Fry. Even if it meant lying to the whole world.

Cameron

"Blaine! Pay attention!" I called from my sprawled position on the floor.

I was lying underneath the folded metal riser we were setting up onstage for the contestants. One end wasn't popping up correctly, so I was trying to push it upright from below while Blaine pulled from the top. Only Blaine was too distracted by Mayor Witherspoon's conversation with Aunt Lenore.

"Blaine!" I shouted again. "You're lifting in the wrong place!"

"*Shhh!* He's talking about who's going to be grand marshal," Blaine scolded me.

As I tried to lift the top riser into place—without Blaine's help—Mayor Witherspoon's deep voice cut through my pounding. "No, Lenore. I haven't decided yet. Besides, even if I had picked someone, I'm not supposed to tell. Right?"

142

"Now, Harvey," Aunt Lenore chided. "You know I wouldn't tell a soul."

"It's me," Blaine whispered above me. "I know it's me. Otherwise he'd tell her." He absentmindedly leaned against the riser, pushing it back down the inch or two I'd just managed to raise it.

"Blaine!" I quickly scrambled out from under the steps and pointed to the other folded riser at the opposite end of the stage. "Look, I can do this one myself. Why don't you go set up the other one?"

"That's a good idea, Blaine, honey," Aunt Lenore added as she walked up to inspect our work. "It would save time too."

"Yeah, Blaine. You don't need an old codger like me to come help, now, do you?" the mayor teased.

I watched Blaine put on his all-American-boy expression. "No, sir, Mr. Witherspoon," he said, jogging over to the collapsed riser as if he'd been waiting all his life to work on it. I mentally thanked the mayor.

Meanwhile I grabbed a wrench nearby and scooted back underneath my steps. Using the wrench as a battering ram, I proceeded to bang the wedged step back into place. My neck was strained and my hands hurt, but I knew as soon as I finished this one last job, we'd be done.

"There you are, Dad! I've been looking all over for you!" came Ashleigh's voice.

I paused in my hammering and peeked through the steps' steel supports. Ashleigh stood chatting with her father, looking beautiful in shorts and a spaghetti-strap halter. *Don't leave,* I willed mentally. *Please don't go yet.*

Ever since I'd awakened from my dream about Uncle Bert, I'd been waiting for a chance to talk to her, but I'd been too busy. Now I was more determined than ever to ask her to the Fall Fest dance, if it wasn't already too late.

Finally I felt the top platform pop into its correct position. I twisted the right screws to lock it into place and double-checked my work. Then I quickly hopped off the stage and approached Ashleigh.

"Hi, Cam!" she said, smiling.

"Hey, Ash," I replied. "Could I, um, talk with you for a sec?"

Her eyebrows knitted together in a cute wavy pattern. "Sure. What's up?"

I glanced around us. Aunt Lenore and Mayor Witherspoon were in a deep discussion about the festival. But I could tell by the way Blaine fiddled with the wrong latches on the riser that he was trying to listen in.

"Why don't we go over here?" I suggested, motioning toward the back of the room.

"Okay."

Once we made our way into the darker section of the ballroom, I turned to face Ashleigh. She was staring at me expectantly. For a second or two I just took in the vision of her. Her face was all shadowy, but the light from the stage bounced off her blond hair, making her look like a heavenly apparition. Suddenly the rest of the world seemed far off.

I sucked in my breath and launched the words out of me. "Ash, I know this is awfully late notice, but I was wondering if maybe, if you don't already have a date, you might want to go to the Fall Fest dance with me?"

It was probably only a fraction of a second before she responded, but it felt like several generations went by. "I'd love to!" she replied, her wide grin gleaming in the half-light.

My mind kept shouting, *She said yes! She said yes!* and I had to remind myself to start breathing again.

"That's great," I gasped. I didn't know what else to say. I'd never fully believed I'd get this far.

Just then Mayor Witherspoon lumbered toward us. "It's time to go, Ashleigh," he called.

"Dad, guess what!" Ashleigh said cheerily. "Cam's taking me to the dance tomorrow night!"

"Glad to hear it," he said. He grabbed my hand and pumped it up and down like a jack handle. "And I want to say how much I appreciate all of your hard work with the pageant."

"Yes," Aunt Lenore chimed in as if it just occurred to her. "I couldn't have done it without you."

"Well, now. We ought to get going," Mayor Witherspoon said to Ashleigh.

"I'll walk out with you two," I said.

Suddenly Blaine bounded up to us, his Reeboks pounding loudly against the wooden floor. "Hey, I'll come too," he announced.

I looked over at the riser he'd been working on. "Are you done already?" I asked incredulously.

"Yeah," Blaine answered, dusting himself off.

"Are you sure? 'Cause those locking bolts can—"

"I'm sure," Blaine said irritably. "Just because I'm faster than you doesn't mean I don't know how to do it. I can fix things too, you know." He pushed past me and jogged to catch up with Mayor Witherspoon, who had already stepped out into the hall with Aunt Lenore.

"What was that all about?" Ashleigh asked.

"I think he's in a hurry to ask your dad to the dance," I replied.

Ashleigh laughed that musical laugh of hers and pushed me lightly. "Speaking of which," she said. "I'm really happy you asked me."

I stared into her wide smile. Again the light from the stage blurred boundaries, making everything in soft focus. I felt like I had stepped into a dream. "Well, I thought about giving you another anonymous heart-shaped box of chocolates," I said, looking down at our shadows on the wood floor, "but I decided against it."

"Oh, really? What changed your mind?"

My memory flooded with images from my dream. "Let's just say . . . I finally woke up."

Instant Message

To: MrKlingon
From: GwenDarby
Subject: Re: Ready for tomorrow?

Doyle,

Ready as I'll ever be. Rehearsal went well except that my car got a flat. Luckily Tony Etheridge came by and gave me a ride. You know, he was really nice. I think you guys might be wrong about him.

—Gwen

To: GwenDarby
From: MrKlingon
Subject: Get real

Hmmm. Car just happens to get a flat and Tony just happens to swing by in time to rescue you? Sounds a little too convenient to me. Remember, Bree has lots of lackeys to do her bidding, and she's wanted this title for a *long* time. She's not going to let anything stand in her way.

So *be careful*.

—Doyle

Twelve

Cameron

I STARED AT the obvious loser in the mirror. The guy was trying to get dressed up, but he only succeeded in looking like he'd just been released from prison. His blazer was one size too small and two fads out of style. His shirt had a faint brown stain between the second and third button. And his ankles poked out from underneath his trousers. The worst part was, the guy was me.

The night before, when Ashleigh said she'd go to the dance with me, I was beyond thrilled. I was so happy, I thought I'd never come back down. But now reality was staring me in the face. All this time I'd worried about asking her, I never once considered that I had nothing to wear.

Basically my entire wardrobe consisted of blue jeans that, to some degree or other, were losing color and structural integrity. My shirts weren't much better. And the only suit I owned was the one I was wearing. I'd never gone to the Fall Fest dance before, but from what I understood, you just *had* to dress up. Plus after listening to Tiffany, I knew that if I wore the wrong thing, I'd embarrass Ashleigh. She certainly didn't deserve that.

There was just one thing to do: call Ashleigh and fake a severe gastrointestinal illness. That way she wouldn't be humiliated, and I could save face by not having to admit being so wardrobe challenged.

I sat down on the bed and held my head in my hands. *Just do it now and get it over with,* I told myself. I took a deep breath and was all set to reach for the phone on the nightstand when something caught my eye. A framed photo of Uncle Bert sat on the top. He was smiling that quiet smile of his—just like in my dream.

"Sorry, Uncle Bert," I mumbled. "I tried."

"Talking to Bert?" Aunt Lenore's voice startled me. I turned my head and saw her standing in the doorway to the guest room. "I talk to him all the time. But I thought I was the only one."

"I just . . ." I paused and stared back down at the picture. "I just miss him."

Aunt Lenore sat down beside me and patted my shoulder. "I know. You two were always so close. He always said you reminded him of himself."

My throat constricted, and warm tears coated my eyes, making Uncle Bert's image go all blurry. I could hear Aunt Lenore sniffling next to me. For a moment we said nothing.

"Goodness, look at the time," Aunt Lenore said, hopping back onto her feet. "I've got to get to the club. And shouldn't you be getting ready for the dance?"

"I'm not going," I grumbled.

"Not going?" she repeated incredulously. "Why not?"

I swallowed hard and stared down at the floor. "I . . . um . . . I don't feel well. I think it's some sort of virus."

Aunt Lenore placed her hand against my forehead, tapping me on the skull with her heavy rings. "You really are like Bert," she said. "Both of you are terrible liars." She grabbed my chin and lifted my face to meet hers. "Now, why don't you tell me why you *really* don't want to go."

Suddenly I felt like a three-year-old. Before I had a chance to think, I ducked my head guiltily and mumbled, "I don't have anything to wear."

Aunt Lenore released her grip and took a step back. Neither of us said a word. I hung my head and contemplated the bedspread while she tapped her toe against the floor. I couldn't remember ever feeling so miserable.

All of a sudden she spun around on her heels and trotted out of the room. "I'll be right back!" she called.

When she returned, she had three plastic-draped outfits slung over her shoulder. She set them down on the bed beside me and tore off the wrapping to reveal three men's suits—expensive ones by the look of them.

I stood and moved back a little as she diligently arranged the clothes. "What's this?" I asked.

"These were in the back of Blaine's closet. I know you two are the same size." She took a navy blazer off its hanger and held it up in front of me.

"Oh no," I protested, holding up my hands. "Thanks, Aunt Lenore, but I can't borrow Blaine's clothes."

"Nonsense!" she exclaimed. "This isn't a loan. I'm giving you one of these suits. And actually these are more *my* suits than Blaine's. After all, I paid for them."

I shook my head vigorously. "No. It's okay. You don't have to do this." I kept backing up, but Aunt Lenore kept following, all the while trying to put that dang jacket on me.

"Just hold still and try this," she urged.

"No. Really, Aunt Lenore. I don't need your help."

"Stop it!" she yelled suddenly, stamping her foot.

I froze, staring at her wide-eyed.

"You are just too full of that Gallagher pride," she went on. "This isn't charity. This is payment for all the help you've given me lately. Now, choose one of these suits, put it on, and go pick up Miss Witherspoon before she thinks she's been stood up!"

Looking at Aunt Lenore's determined face, I saw something I'd never seen before. I saw the young lady, so full of courage and spirit, that Uncle Bert fell in love with. Uncle Bert used to always say he could never win an argument with her. I certainly wasn't about to try.

"All right," I said, smiling slightly. "I'll try them on."

"Good." Aunt Lenore gave a nod, thrust the navy jacket into my hands, and headed for the door. "Oh," she said, turning back around. "One more thing."

"What's that?" I asked.

Aunt Lenore pulled her car keys out of her skirt pocket and tossed them to me. "Drop me off at the club and take my car to pick up Ashleigh. I'll get a ride home with Blaine."

"But . . . ," I started protesting.

"Now, now," Aunt Lenore said, holding up a hand. "You don't want Ashleigh's dress getting all wrinkled in that Volkswagen, do you?"

I stared at her, unable to speak. I wanted to find a way to tell her how incredibly grateful I was, but I just couldn't find the words.

"Aunt Lenore, I . . . I . . ."

But after all those years with Uncle Bert, Aunt Lenore must have learned a thing or two about us Gallaghers. She beamed at me and said, "You're welcome, Cameron," then turned and disappeared out the door.

Marissa

I stood looking out my bedroom window. Fry was out there. He was sitting on the roof of his carport again, drinking root beer and sketching. I wanted so badly to go over there or at least open the window and call to him. Funny. It had only been one day, and I already missed him.

"Hey, sweetheart. What're you doing tonight?" my dad asked as he stepped into my room.

I whirled around. "Nothing," I replied a little too quickly.

Dad peered past me out the window. "I don't believe it. Do you see what that hoodlum is doing?" he grumbled. "Drinking beer in full daylight, where anyone can see."

"Maybe it's not beer," I said curtly.

Dad frowned. "I know what I saw. Do you think it's cool what he's doing? What if some kids were out there watching him, and they decided it would be cool for them to drink beer too?"

"Dad, you're not making any sense! You don't even know him!"

His eyes grew wide. "Do you? A couple of days of painting pictures and you're suddenly that hairy beast's best friend?"

I wanted to yell, "Yes! I am his friend! And he's not some beast. He's the most incredible person in this backward town!" But I couldn't. My dad's face was already fire-truck red. If I told him how I felt about Fry, who knew what it would do to him.

"Marissa? Do you have something to say to me?" My dad's voice was loud and panicky.

I couldn't stand it anymore. I walked past him and raced down the stairs. Mom was sitting in the living room, reading.

"Mom, can I borrow your car?" I asked.

"Sure, honey." She gestured to her keys on the foyer table. "Are you going to the pageant?"

"God, no," I said, wrinkling my upper lip.

By now my dad had caught up with me. "Where are you going?" he asked suspiciously.

"I don't know! To the movies, probably. I just want to get out of here!"

Mom and Dad exchanged looks.

"Please!" I pleaded.

"Do we have your word that you're just going to the movies?" he asked, peering into my eyes.

"Yes!"

"Okay, then." He nodded and made a slight gesture toward the door.

Finally, I thought. I grabbed the keys off the table and hurried outside before Dad changed his mind.

As I walked over to Mom's Camry, I looked up at Fry. I wanted to at least wave to him, but he didn't seem to notice me. Oh, well. No sense riling up Dad again when I barely got out of there to begin with.

I got in the car and started driving to the Kingstown 8 Cineplex—the only movie theater in town. But when I pulled into the empty parking lot, I noticed a paper sign taped to the door of the theater. Closed for Fall Fest, it read. I could barely believe it. The entire town was shutting down for this stupid festival. Now what?

I drove around for a few minutes, but everything else was closed too. In the meantime a steady stream of cars passed me, heading for the country club.

Eventually I turned around and headed that way too. I figured it wouldn't hurt to go for a little while. And I certainly didn't want to head home yet.

By the time I got there, it was so packed, I had to pull into a parking space near the rear of the building. I got out of the car and locked it, glancing all around me. I was just thinking about how my dad would never approve of my choosing such a dark section of the lot, near a bunch of trees that weirdos could lurk behind, when someone suddenly stepped out of the shadows toward me.

"Hey, Marissa," the figure said.

It was Fry.

"Hey. What are you doing here?" I said, trying not to sound panicked.

"I came to see my sister," he explained. "My folks are busy directing a play down at the college, so I'm the only one who can come support her."

"Oh. Right," I said.

"Also, I saw you leave your house and figured you might show up here. So I've been keeping a lookout for your car." He leaned against the Camry and bounced his right foot on the asphalt. "It's weird, you know. I kind of miss working on that stupid backdrop."

I smiled. "Me too."

We stared at each other for a moment, grinning secretive grins. As I looked through his unkempt hair into his eyes, a quiet feeling came over me— that relaxed, happy feeling you get when you come home after a hard day. I never felt that way in my own house anymore. I never felt it anywhere, except now with Fry.

"The pageant's about to begin!" called some white-suited waiter walking through the parking lot. "Ten more minutes!"

Fry nodded toward the club. "What do you say? You want to go in and see our work?"

"Sure," I replied. "Let's go."

Gwenyth

So far, so good, I thought as I changed into my dance outfit in the dressing room. Onstage, Tracy Reed began warbling a Sarah McLachlan tune at the top of her lungs. It was the beginning of the talent portion, and I was thankful I was going last. That would give me plenty of time to prepare.

Amazingly, I already felt worn out. So far all we had done was introduce ourselves to the audience and stand in a line, smiling, while Mrs. Gallagher talked for eight minutes just welcoming everyone to the show. I thought my cheek muscles were going to spasm. I tried to scan the crowd for Tony, but the lights were too bright and my eyes were glazed over from not blinking enough.

From here on out, I would never make fun of pageant contestants again. I never realized what hard work it was.

"Gwenyth! Gwenyth Darby!" I heard Mrs. Gallagher call.

I quickly stepped out from behind the changing screen. "Right here," I answered.

"There's going to be a slight change of plans," Mrs. Gallagher said, scurrying over to me. "Since it takes so long to get the piano on and off the stage, we're going to have Linda perform last. So we're up to you or Bree. Do you think you can go next, after Tracy?"

"Uh . . . sure," I replied.

"Oh, good!" She pressed her clipboard against her and hugged herself. "I'll go tell Bree she's on after you, and I'll let the sound operator know you've brought your own music. Be sure and give him your tape or CD on your way to the stage."

"Okay."

Mrs. Gallagher opened the door and cupped a hand over her ear. "It sounds like Tracy's finishing up. Just a couple more minutes and you should head backstage," she said, gesturing behind her. Then she stepped out and shut the door.

Great. Here I thought I had twenty minutes to get ready and I only had two. I tied on my ballet slippers and quickly stretched my legs. Bree sat at the nearby dressing table, putting yet another layer of makeup on her face. I could see her reflection in the mirror, smirking at me. *Yeah, yeah. Save it for the judges,* I thought.

One more minute to go. I leaped to my feet and rummaged through my gym bag for my music CD, only it wasn't in the side zipper pocket where I always kept it. I hurriedly emptied the bag onto the floor and picked through the contents, but it was nowhere.

Oh God! I panicked. *How could I be so irresponsible?*

"Has anyone seen my CD?" I asked.

Everyone in the room looked at me and shook their heads. Everyone except Bree. She sat brushing her hair and casually staring up at the ceiling, but her lips were pursed together as if she were trying to stop from laughing. I knew right then that I shouldn't even bother searching for the CD.

"Everyone's clapping. I think Tracy's done," Linda said, listening at the door. "You should get out there, Gwen."

I stood paralyzed, wondering what to do. It would be useless to try and confront Bree. She'd be smart enough to cover her tracks. And running to Mrs. Gallagher wouldn't help either. All she cared about was making sure the show went on as scheduled. So what then? Did I bore the audience with my sob story? Did I pull out of the competition?

At that moment the laughter Bree was holding back must have overtaken her. She made a small snort and then innocently stared off into the distance.

I'll show her, I thought. I tapped into my anger and felt myself refilling with strength. Holding my head high, I walked out of the room and headed backstage.

Mrs. Gallagher was already onstage. As soon as she saw me, she smiled and nodded—obviously unaware that I hadn't given my music to the sound guy. "And now," she announced, stepping up to the microphone, "dancing to the tune of Vivaldi's *Four Seasons,* we have Miss Gwenyth Darby." She made a dramatic flourish and exited in the opposite direction.

Here goes nothing, I thought. I calmly walked to the center of the stage. Standing in third position, I shut my eyes and searched for the "zone" I always lapse into when I perform. As soon as I felt it, I began the routine.

At first it was a little strange. Even though I was totally concentrating on what I was doing, I could still hear some confused murmurs coming up from the crowd. I was listening to the music in my head, but I knew it must be weird for them. All they could hear were my feet sliding and pounding against the stage.

All of a sudden a rhythmic clapping started up somewhere in the audience. Out of the corner of my eye I could see Doyle and the gang sitting up front, clapping in perfect time to the unheard music. Gradually everyone joined in until the entire audience was marking out my rhythm for me. It was so cool. The entire place seemed to get fired up—a few people even tried to whistle or hum the melody by memory.

When I finally finished, the whole crowd exploded into applause. I was thrown by how enthusiastic they were. In all my years of dance, I'd never heard a reaction like that. I looked over at my friends and smiled gratefully.

For some reason, it was important for me to see Tony. I started scanning the faces, but before I could find him, Mrs. Gallagher came out and reminded the audience who I was. After a quick bow I turned and ran offstage.

The rest of the girls were waiting in the wings.

"Wow, Gwen. That was incredible!" Linda cried.

"Yeah," Tracy said. "You were really good."

"Thanks," I replied, trying to catch my breath.

Just then I caught sight of Bree standing off to the side. Her smug smile was gone. As soon as she saw me, her face gave a strange little twitch. Then she whirled around and marched back to the dressing room.

She looked so stressed, I almost felt sorry for her. *Almost*.

Beep! *You have reached Lenny Pipkin's ultraprivate phone line. I'm not around right now, but leave a message or I'll come looking for ya. Beep!*

Hey, Lenny. It's Will. I've just been talking with Blaine, and I've got an idea. Meet me at the club tonight and bring your tools. This is going to be good.

Thirteen

Marissa

"YOUR SISTER DID great!" I whispered, elbowing Fry. "That was so original, to dance without music."

"I wouldn't be too sure that was her idea," Fry muttered. "I wouldn't put it past one of her competitors to have stolen her music."

"Me either," I said. "Still, she was awesome. I'll bet you anything she wins. That'll show those stuck-up snots."

Fry smiled proudly.

It was bizarre. If someone had told me just the day before that I would have fun at a beauty pageant, I'd have laughed myself breathless. But here I was, having a ball.

Fry and I were standing along the back wall instead of sitting in the folding chairs with everyone else. It was partly because we came in late and almost all the seats were taken. But mainly it was because we didn't want to be part of the crowd. This way we could be aloof and cool and have our private little conversations.

"The backdrop looks good, doesn't it?" he said, sounding a little surprised.

"Yeah," I agreed. It did look great under the lights, especially the deep indigo of the night sky and all the tiny gold stars. I remembered our little paint fight and smiled to myself. If only we could have another moment like that. If only my dad didn't have to spoil everything.

"Man, this girl is annoying," Fry said, pointing at the stage.

It was Bree Hampton's turn for the talent competition, and she really was over the top. She was doing a cutesy tumbling routine to the Kingstown High School song and firing up the crowd with pep-rally cheers. The girl was milking it for all she could get.

"Who is this chick?" Fry grumbled. "Let me check the program."

I was just about to tell him it was Bree Hampton when I noticed a man stand up in the audience and sidestep down his row toward the main aisle. It was my dad.

What's he doing here? I wondered, trembling with panic. *Didn't I just leave him at home?*

I glanced at his empty chair and saw the back of Mom's head in the next seat over. After I left home, they must have decided to come watch the show.

Or maybe they had planned to all along.

Dad reached the main aisle and was headed our way, probably going on a bathroom break. Every cell in my body quaked with fear. There was no way I could let him see me. For one thing, he didn't even know I was here; I'd promised him I'd be at the movies. And for another thing—this one much worse—if he saw me with Fry, the entire town would end up witnessing a double homicide. But I was trapped. If I tried to leave now, he'd see me for sure.

I glanced over at Fry to see if he'd noticed my dad, but he was still squinting down at his program. Meanwhile Dad just kept coming closer and closer. A few more feet and I'd easily be in range of his sight.

My pulse sped up to supersonic levels. My breathing stopped. Just when I was about to throw myself into my father's path and beg forgiveness, I heard someone call his name.

Dad stopped and turned to face the person. It was old Mr. Hubert, sitting at the end of the back row. I could hear him whispering loudly to Dad, asking him how he was feeling.

As soon as Dad's back was to me, I saw a chance to escape.

"I'm going to go get a drink," I said to Fry.

"What?" he mumbled, without looking up.

But I was already heading out the exit. I felt bad about racing away like that, but there was just no time to explain. As fast as I could, I hurried through the lobby and out the front door into the parking lot.

Once I was safely outside, I breathed a sigh of

relief. That had been close. Of course, now I had a new problem. I had no idea when or how or even *if* I should go back inside. If I didn't return, Fry would think I was blowing him off. But if I did, I'd run the risk of Dad catching me again.

Why does it all have to be so hard? I thought, leaning against the low stone wall. Lately it seemed like every part of my life was confusing. I wanted so much but had no idea how to make it all happen. I wanted my dad to be healthy again and go back to his old, easygoing self. I wanted everyone at school to stop being so phony. And I wanted so badly to be with Fry, without having to worry all the time.

Right now none of those things seemed possible.

Clang! Clunk! Chiiiing! A series of strange sounds emanated from the dark parking lot. Figuring I had nothing else to do, I crept around the wall and walked along the edge of the yard to investigate. As I neared the rear of the building, I could hear people talking in hushed tones.

"Give me the pliers, Lenny."

"I don't have any."

"I told you to bring some! How the heck are we supposed to do this without pliers?"

"Beats me. It was your great idea, Will."

Will Benson! I thought I recognized his voice. I reached the far end of the wall and peered around the corner. Sure enough, there stood Will and Lenny. They were crouched down next to a motorcycle, doing something. Looking closer, I realized it was Fry's Kawasaki. Red-hot rage bubbled up inside me. Obviously they were pulling some juvenile prank—probably trying to give Fry a flat.

"What do you guys think you're doing?" I called out, emerging from the shadows.

At first they jumped at the sound of me. Then Will said, "Aw, man. It's just Marissa."

"I mean it, Will. What are you up to?" I demanded.

Will grinned mischievously and stepped aside so I could see their handiwork. On the ground next to the motorcycle was a thick metal chain attached to a mailbox. The other end of the chain Lenny was attaching to the rear of the bike.

"What the . . . ?" I sputtered.

"Cool, isn't it?" Will said, nudging me with his elbow. "Actually you gave us the idea. You told Blaine your dad thought Fry was the one smashing the mailboxes. So now we're going to link him to our crime—in front of the whole town." He bobbed his head up and down and yukked to himself.

"Yeah," Lenny chimed in. "As soon as we get it on the bike, we're going to run in and tell everyone what we found. Then we'll be off the hook."

"No, you won't!" I cried, suddenly finding my voice. "No way will I let you get away with this. I'm going to tell them what you're doing!"

I turned in a huff and started marching back toward the club, but Will stopped me. He grabbed my arm and spun me around to face him.

"No, you're not," he said, his face cruel and scared at the same time. "You aren't going anywhere."

Gwenyth

The lights onstage dimmed, and the audience clapped appreciatively. While Mrs. Gallagher announced intermission, we eight girls turned and tromped offstage single file, all the way back to the dressing room.

Okay, so that *made me feel like a show horse,* I thought as I plopped into one of the chairs and kicked off my heels. The evening-gown competition was probably the hardest so far. Mainly it consisted of smiling and turning to the left, smiling more and turning to the right, smiling while turning around in a slow circle, and then heading back to the line of grinning contestants. Then, while everyone else took a turn, we had to stand still and smile, smile, smile some more. After a while my face went numb. I wondered if my features could become permanently jammed into that position.

At least it was almost over. After intermission they would announce the winner. So far, I had no clue who it could be. I couldn't even begin to guess how I was doing.

A knock sounded on the dressing-room door, sending five half-undressed contestants squealing behind the folding screen.

"I'll get it," Bree said, rolling her eyes. She opened up the door, and there stood one of the club's busboys.

"Hello," he said nervously with a Spanish accent. "You do the . . . ?" He made his hands do a flipping, twirling motion.

"Oh, you mean my routine? Yes, that was me," Bree replied.

"Ah, *bueno*. These for you." The man reached behind him and lifted up a gigantic bouquet of fresh flowers.

"Omigod!" Bree exclaimed. "For me?"

The man nodded, pointed at the card tied to the glass vase, and left.

As soon as the door shut, the other girls emerged from behind the screen. "Who is it from, Bree? Who sent them?" they demanded. I was just as curious, but I didn't say anything.

Bree waved them off. "Just wait. Give me a chance to read it." She opened the tiny yellow envelope and pulled out the card. As she read, a soft glow came over her face.

"Well?" Tracy asked, bouncing impatiently.

Bree held up the card for all to see. "It's from Tony," she announced triumphantly.

Tony? Tony Etheridge? I tried to act nonchalant, but deep down my heart was turning inside out. *It isn't true,* I told myself. *Tony said he couldn't stand her. Why would he send her flowers?*

"You are so lucky, Bree," Linda Loftin swooned as she plucked the card out of Bree's hands. "Look at this. He wrote, 'All my love, Tony.' Isn't that romantic?"

Suddenly it felt like a jagged knife was ripping through my chest. While the rest of the girls crowded around Bree, oohing and aahing at the bouquet, I disappeared behind the changing screen. No way was I giving Bree the satisfaction of seeing me upset.

So it's true, I thought, quickly wiping a renegade tear off my cheek. *Tony sent her flowers. But if he's in love with her, why would he lead me on like that?*

Doyle's recent warning flashed into my mind. "Bree has lots of lackeys to do her bidding. . . ." Was Tony in cahoots with her? Did she convince him to play me like that just to mess with my mind? No, it was too cruel. I could easily believe she would do such a thing, but Tony? Not him. *Please don't let it be true of him.*

And yet it was the only thing that made sense. He had always been there at weird times. First at the library. Then at the club when my tire went flat. I'd just assumed it was coincidence—that unlike in New York, people in small towns were always running into each other. Now it seemed so obvious I was set up. How could I have been so stupid? I could just imagine how they'd laugh about all this later on at the dance.

Let them laugh, I thought, taking a deep breath and forcing back the tears. This was probably just some ploy of theirs to make me pull out of the contest. Well, I wasn't going to. Even if Bree won the crown *and* Tony, I would stand there and take it with a big, aching smile. No one made a fool out of Gwen Darby.

Except maybe Gwen Darby.

Cameron

I know it sounds clichéd, but I had to be the happiest guy to have ever walked the planet. The night was going so well. I had decent clothes, a decent borrowed car, and the most beautiful girl in the galaxy on my arm.

When Ashleigh had opened up the door to her house, I gasped at the sight of her. She was wearing this soft-looking, peach-colored dress that showed off her lightly bronzed skin. And her hair was twisted up in this loose knot with wispy strands hanging down her face. It blew my mind that I was actually taking her out.

Then when we arrived at the club, she grabbed my hand as we walked into the ballroom. And all through the first part of the pageant we talked and laughed as if we'd been together forever. Everything felt almost magical. I couldn't wait to hold her at the dance later on.

"So who do you think is going to win?" Ashleigh asked me as we walked around during intermission.

"I have no idea," I replied. "That girl Gwen was great, and Linda is a really good piano player. But Bree probably got to the judges with all that pro-Kingstown stuff."

"I thought that was a bit much," Ashleigh said, wrinkling her nose. "I mean, it was just too obvious a play for votes. I hope Gwen wins. I don't know. She just seemed the nicest."

I reached down and grabbed her hand—it was amazing how natural it felt now—and we continued to walk around the lobby, looking at the paintings on the wall. A couple of times Ash would lean against me or tilt her head against my shoulder, making me go almost dizzy with emotion.

"Would you like a soda?" I asked.

"Sure," she replied. "Thanks."

"Okay. Be back in a sec." I let my eyes linger on her for a while, then turned and headed toward the bar. It amazed me that I actually had to walk there when I had the distinct feeling I could fly through the air if I tried.

A stressed-out-looking bartender took my order and moved down to the far end. While I waited for him to return, I turned around and leaned back against the bar. I knew I still had a big, dippy smile on my face, but I couldn't help it.

Just then Blaine emerged from a nearby crowd of people and stalked right up to me. "What are you trying to do?" he demanded, his face twisted into a scowl.

"Uh . . . hi, Blaine," I replied, still smiling. Not even he could ruin the mood. "What are you talking about?"

"Don't play dumb with me. My mom just told me I'm supposed to give her a ride home."

"So?" I asked, not quite getting his point.

"So, you did that on purpose! I'm probably going to be named grand marshal tonight, and you couldn't stand it. So you made sure I wouldn't be able to hang around and get all the attention, didn't you?"

I shook my head. "You're wigging," I said. "Your mom just loaned me her car as a favor. I didn't even ask for it."

Blaine curled his upper lip. "Don't give me that.

Mom never loans out her Beemer. What makes you so special?"

"Gee, I don't know," I replied sarcastically. "Maybe she was grateful that I actually help her out once in a while?"

Suddenly it was as if a shade had been drawn behind Blaine's eyes, making his expression dark and cold. "You think you're so great, don't you?" he hissed. "Just because Dad always liked you better, you think you can sucker up to my mom and become her favorite. Well, forget it! I'm on to you, mama's boy."

I leaned there, totally stunned. It had never, ever occurred to me that Blaine felt this way.

"Hey, Blaine. It's not like that. Really. All I meant was—"

"Wait a sec," Blaine interrupted, grabbing my jacket collar. "You're wearing my clothes!"

"Yeah. I mean, no. Your mom said I could have it."

But Blaine just ignored me. "I can't believe you took this without permission! Who do you think you are? First you muscle in on my family and now this? You are so low."

"No. I'm not." I shook my head vigorously. "Just hear me out."

"No way, brownnoser. The free ride is over." Blaine stuck his face an inch away from mine and smiled coldly. "If you don't get out of here in the next ten minutes, I'll go tell Ashleigh you're a big phony who steals people's clothes."

"What?" I said, chuckling nervously. "No way."

"I mean it," he added. "Nine minutes and fifty-five seconds."

A helpless feeling shot through me. "Blaine! You know I can't do that! She's my date."

"So what," he said, smirking. "She's not a real date. The only reason she's going out with you is because she feels sorry for you. Poor mechanic's son Cameron with a hurt mommy."

I had to rein in the urge to punch him in the face. "You are so wrong," I said, clenching my jaw.

"Oh yeah? How many times has she asked you about your mom?"

I paused. She had asked about her a few times. But that was just because she was nice. Right?

Blaine threw back his head and cackled. "Yeah, just like I thought. You're just a charity case. When you asked her out, she didn't want to hurt your feelings by saying no."

An icy sensation poured through me, stiffening my back and hardening my hands into fists. "No!" I said. "It's not true!"

"Nine minutes," he said, casually glancing at his watch. "I suggest you go tell Ashleigh she needs to find another ride."

Fourteen

Marissa

"DON'T DO ANYTHING stupid, Marissa," Will said, still grabbing my upper arms and pulling me backward.

"Let me go!" I shouted. By now I wasn't angry anymore, just scared.

Will stood behind me with a firm lock on the back of my arms. I twisted around and tried to break his hold, but he was too strong. All I could manage was a few backward kicks that had no effect at all.

"Stop it, Will! You're hurting me!" I cried.

"Uh-uh," he snarled right into my ear. "Not until we know you aren't going to turn us in."

I continued struggling in his grip, and we lurched around the edge of the parking lot in a weird sort of dance. My arms were aching, and hot tears mixed with eye makeup stung my eyes.

I can't give in, I told myself. *He can't get away with this!*

"Leave her alone!" someone suddenly yelled. I couldn't see him, but I could tell it was Fry.

The next thing I knew, there was a rumbling of footsteps and an extra pair of arms wedged in between me and Will. I ended up being catapulted off to the side, landing on my knees against the asphalt.

I looked up and saw Fry and Will tangled up together. Fry's face was all red, and his eyes blazed furiously. Will didn't seem to know what was going on. In no time Fry had Will in a choke hold with his right arm pinned behind his back.

"If you ever touch her again," Fry growled, "I will rip your head off!"

Lenny stood a few feet behind them, his eyes and mouth wide with shock. But as soon as Fry's back was turned, he started to creep up behind him.

"Stop!" I hollered. Without even thinking, I picked up a nearby wrench and ran toward Lenny, threatening to beam him on the forehead.

"Whoa. Whoa," he said, holding his hands up in front of him.

Suddenly more voices sounded from the side yard. I looked up and saw Henry, the security guard, racing across the grass, followed by two waiters.

"Break it up! Break it up!" Henry shouted, forcing his small frame between Will and Fry. One waiter pulled Fry off Will while the other stepped in the middle of me and Lenny.

"What do you think you're doing, coming here

and starting up trouble?" Henry hollered at Fry.

"No, Henry!" I cried. "It wasn't him!"

Henry turned around. "Marissa?" he said, squinting at me.

"Those guys were trying to frame him for all the mailbox smashings. Look." I gestured toward the chain Lenny had attached to the back of Fry's bike. "And when I told them I was going to turn them in, they started threatening me. *He* stopped them! He was protecting me!" I pointed at Fry. For a moment our eyes met, and I smiled gratefully at him.

"It's not true!" Will protested. "She's lying!"

Henry kept glancing around, from Fry to the motorcycle to Will and Lenny and then back to me.

"If you don't believe me, just look at their hands." I stalked over to Lenny and lifted his wrist. Grease and grime covered his fingers. Lenny tore his hand away, but not before Henry had a chance to see the evidence.

"All right. Let's take those two up into the office," Henry said to the waiters.

I rushed over to Fry as the waitperson let him go. He smiled at me and ran a hand through my hair. "Are you okay?" he asked.

"I'm fine," I said, smiling back at him.

Will started lurching around as the guys tried to steer him up to the club. "You lied!" he screamed, glaring at me. "I can't believe you're standing up for that freak!"

"Come on, buddy," Henry said, pulling at Will's arm.

"You told Blaine nothing was going on with you and Fry! And you told me you hated him!"

Fry stiffened up and stared at Will. Then he turned back to me with a perplexed expression.

Will noticed Fry's reaction and laughed. "Yeah, that's right. Your girlfriend's a liar. She told me she was only being nice to you so she could get an A in art."

I jumped at the sound of my own words. Fry peered hard at me, and I knew the guilt shone on my face like a fresh coat of paint.

"See! She can't deny it! The liar!" Will called out.

"Be quiet!" Henry ordered, and tightening his grip on Will's arm, he and the waiter finally managed to drag him up the sidewalk and around the corner of the building.

At this point a small crowd of curious onlookers was slowly pouring into the parking lot. They watched eagerly as Will and Lenny were led away, then turned their attention to me and Fry.

But Fry didn't even seem to notice them. He stood staring at me with a look full of hurt and disgust. My throat constricted, and an icy sensation spilled through my veins. I felt like I was drowning in shame.

"I can explain," I whispered hoarsely.

"No," he said, his voice cold and harsh. "Don't bother." He took a couple of steps back from me, then spun around and headed for his motorcycle.

"Wait!" I whimpered. "Please just hear me out!"

But Fry only seemed to walk faster. He reached his Kawasaki and angrily yanked the chain off the back. As he hopped on the bike and started it up, I raced over to his side.

"Please," I pleaded over the noise of the engine. "Please don't go, Fry."

He snapped his head around and glared at me. "Don't call me that!" he growled. "I hate being called that!" And then he noisily sped away.

I stood there, sobbing, as I watched him disappear into the shadows. *What have I done?* I kept asking myself. *How can I ever fix this?*

Cameron

My hands were shaking as I went back to meet Ashleigh at our seats. It's amazing I didn't dump Dr Pepper all over myself.

"Did you see everyone clear out of here?" Ashleigh asked as I reached her. "Someone said there was a fight."

"I didn't notice," I mumbled truthfully. I wouldn't have noticed if an active volcano had burst through the floor of the lobby. For the past few minutes (exactly five and a half, according to Blaine) I'd done nothing but force myself to face the ugly reality of my situation: I had to cut short my perfect date with Ashleigh. If I didn't, Blaine would humiliate me in all sorts of cruel and creative ways. He was like a man possessed. At least if I obeyed his command and broke it off myself, I'd have some control.

"What's wrong?" Ashleigh asked, placing her hand on my arm. "You look sort of out of it."

I tried not to look into her balmy brown eyes. This was hard enough as it was. Taking a deep breath, I launched into the excuse I'd been rehearsing for the past two and a half minutes. "I . . . I need to go home. I have sort of an emergency, but I can't talk about it now." There. I'd done it. At least it wasn't an all-out lie.

"Oh no!" she exclaimed. Her voice was so full of genuine sympathy, I couldn't help but look at her. Her brow was furrowed, and her head was tilted slightly as she peered at me in worry. "Is it your mom?" she asked softly. "Is she okay?"

Suddenly it was as if she'd sloshed her icy soda on me. *Why did she assume it was about Mom?* I wondered. *Is Blaine right? Is she just with me because she feels sorry for me?*

Ashleigh must have noticed my startled reaction. "I'm sorry," she said ruefully. "You said you couldn't talk about it. But I just want you to know that I'm here for you if you want to open up."

She grabbed my hand and squeezed it reassuringly. For some reason, the gesture seemed too maternal, too full of pity. I started to believe Blaine was right. Ashleigh was a wonderful, sweet person. And right now I was her favorite cause.

The sudden realization seemed to jar my heart out of place. It teetered on its perch like an old creaky sign before falling down somewhere around my ankles.

Just then I could see Blaine entering the ballroom.

He slowly scanned the paltry crowd until his eyes settled on us. *Uh-oh,* I thought. *Time's up.*

"Hey, listen," I said quickly. "Can you get another ride home?"

"Uh . . . yeah. I guess," Ashleigh replied.

"Good. I'm really sorry, but I've gotta run."

"Okay . . . ," she said, her face knitted up with confusion. "Are you sure you don't want to talk about—"

But I couldn't stay to hear her out. Blaine was already headed our way. "No. I'm sorry," I said abruptly. "Bye, Ash." Then I turned and sped out of the room—leaving my date, and my dignity, behind me.

Gwenyth

All I wanted now was for this night to be over.

The rest of the contestants and I were standing offstage next to the steps to the winner's platform. The audience seemed restless, the other girls wiggled nervously, and Mrs. Gallagher was yammering into the microphone about how we were coming to the "big moment." You'd think I'd be doubled over with suspense, but I wasn't. Instead I was fighting tears with the trace amounts of energy I had left in me. I wondered how I'd made it out of the dressing room at all.

"Omigod! Omigod! I think I'm going to hyperventilate!" Linda gasped.

"Don't worry," Bree said coolly. "It will be over soon."

I could feel her turn and stare right at me, but there was no way I was going to meet that smug expression again. Since the moment she got Tony's flowers, Bree had done nothing but preen the bouquet and shoot me little looks of triumph.

Funny. I'd thought I entered the pageant in order to prove something to everyone. I'd figured I could show Bree that I wasn't afraid of her and maybe prove that I was just as good as she was. But I was wrong. Obviously Bree was on top for a reason. If she could strut around treating people like dirt and Tony still wanted her, then maybe she really was superior. And if I could still have a thing for Tony, even after everything he pulled on me, then surely I was some sort of lesser being.

"Omigod! I think it's starting!" Linda squealed, hopping up and down.

"Shhh!" went Tracy. "Here comes Mrs. Hoffmeyer."

A trim woman in a long, denim skirt stood up from the front row and walked to the stage to hand Mrs. Gallagher something.

"The judges have given me their envelope, and I will soon be announcing the name of the winner. . . . " Mrs. Gallagher's voice echoed through the auditorium. "But first let me take a moment to thank everyone involved."

The entire audience seemed to grumble collectively. Linda and the others let out impatient groans. Only Bree looked calm. Of course she would. She was going to win. She always got whatever she wanted: Tony, the crown, a bevy of people to do her bidding. Whatever made me think I could break her rules and get away with it? That day I first stood up to her, she'd warned me she'd get even, and she did. Now she could personally see that the rest of my senior year was even more unbearable.

The entire place fell into a hush, but I barely heard Mrs. Gallagher's voice when she said, "And now I would like to present Kingstown's next Fall Festival queen . . . Miss Gwenyth Darby!"

"What?" I mumbled.

"What?" Bree shouted.

"Congratulations!" Linda screeched. She threw her arms around me in a quick hug and then pushed me forward. "Go!" she urged. "Go on up there!"

I *won? She called* my *name?* I kept wondering. I suddenly felt like I'd slipped into one of those alternate realities Rom was always talking about.

In a daze I slowly made my way toward the steps to the winner's platform. I was only vaguely aware of the applause and the other girls hugging and patting me along the way.

"There she is!" Mrs. Gallagher announced as I came forward.

Still in shock, I kept moving forward on autopilot. The clapping and cheers buzzed in my ears, and the winner's platform seemed to loom up for miles. In a dumbstruck trance I lifted my foot to climb the first step and emerge from behind the curtain.

Bree leaned forward as I passed her and stepped on the first level of the riser. "Congratulations," she said coldly.

The next thing I knew, I was soaring through the air. My feet flew upward, and the stage seemed to turn upside down. Then came a loud, crashing sound followed by searing pain in my head and side.

After that, all my senses became jumbled. Sights and noises blurred and became indecipherable, as if I were standing in the center strip of a busy highway. Only an occasional recognizable sound cut through to my brain.

"Omigod! Bree! I can't believe you tripped her!" came Linda's high-pitched shriek.

"I—I didn't mean to," came Bree's scared-sounding reply. "I just wanted to make her stumble."

Rapid footsteps reverberated against the stage floor, stabbing their way into my head. I wanted to yell at them to stop, but I couldn't make myself speak.

"Get back!" said a deep voice. "Someone call for help!"

Then everything swirled down a giant drain until all that remained was quiet blackness.

The Bluebonnet County Register

Mrs. Lenore Gallagher, coordinator of the Fall Festival queen pageant and owner of the Kingstown Country Club, spoke with a 911 operator from her cellular phone after Gwenyth Darby, a pageant contestant, was injured after tripping on a stage prop. Said Mrs. Gallagher, "I hope the public doesn't think this reflects the way we do things here in Kingstown. This is the first accident ever in our pageant's thirty-year history." Ms. Darby's condition was still not known at press time.

Fifteen

Gwenyth

MY EYES OPENED a crack, and all I could see was white. For a second I assumed I had passed on to the Great Beyond. Then I wondered why the Great Beyond reeked of rubbing alcohol.

I blinked open my lids and tried to raise my head, which immediately started throbbing. Now I could see I was in a hospital room, with white walls, a white ceiling, and white sheets covering me up to my shoulders.

"Whoa. Stop. Lie back down." My brother appeared at my side, looking terrible. The skin around his left eye was swollen and reddish purple, and there were several tiny scrapes and gashes on his cheeks.

"What happened to you?" I croaked.

"Forget me," Brian snapped. "You're the one I'm worried about."

I slowly raised a hand to my aching forehead. "What happened to me?"

Brian blew his breath out of his mouth and shook his head angrily. "That prima donna Bree tripped you as you were going up the stairs for the crown, and the whole thing collapsed. Apparently it wasn't set up right." He looked down at me, his features creasing up with worry. "You passed out. The doctors say you have a slight concussion and your right shoulder was dislocated."

I stared past him, trying to remember it all. "Bree tripped me?"

"Yeah," he said, his jaw muscles starting to twitch. "Man, if only I'd been there! I'd have ripped her apart."

"You weren't there?" I asked.

Brian's face fell guiltily. "No." His hands kneaded the side railing of my bed as if it were a lump of clay. "Sorry I missed your big moment. I . . . I sort of had to leave before it was over. Thank God Doyle reached me at home."

He looked so out of it. I knew there was something else going on that he wasn't telling me. "What happened, Bri? Why are you all beat up?"

"I'll tell you later," he said, reaching over to grab my nose. "Let's just say it was a real bad night for the Darbys."

A knock sounded on the door. "Hey. Is she awake?" came Doyle's whispered voice.

"Yeah," Brian answered. He turned back to me. "The guys have been waiting to see you. I'm going to go tell Mom and Dad you're awake. They're in the waiting room, talking to the doctor."

"Okay."

As Brian's shaggy head disappeared out the doorway, Doyle, Rom, Haskell, Oscar, Bennett, Larry, and Terry trotted into the room single file, each one wearing an expression of concern.

"You feeling better?" Bennett asked.

"Yeah. Thanks," I replied. "And thanks for your help at the pageant. I couldn't have gotten through it without you."

"You did great, Gwen," Doyle said.

"Yeah!" Oscar echoed. "You rocked!"

"Man!" Haskell exclaimed. "I'd have given anything to see the look on Bree's face when they said you won!"

"Which reminds me," Doyle interrupted. "I sort of have some bad news." He looked around at the others, and one by one their faces sagged. "Since the accident has left you unable to fulfill your duties as Fall Festival queen, they had to give the title to someone else."

"Oh," I said. I took a few seconds to search my feelings and realized I wasn't at all upset. In fact, I was slightly relieved. "Who got it?"

"Well . . . it was supposed to go to the first runner-up, which was Bree," Doyle explained. "But she was disqualified for tripping you, so it went to the second runner-up—Linda Loftin, which infuriated Bree to no end. In fact, the only reason Bree actually let her pal Linda compete in the pageant was because Bree was sure she'd beat her."

I rolled my eyes, which hurt a little. "I'm glad for Linda. She'll be great. You know, it really wouldn't have felt right to take the crown after basically cheating to get in."

Doyle made a noise as if he were going to protest, but I held up a shaky hand.

"Plus I was running for the wrong reasons anyway," I added. "I didn't want to be queen; I wanted to show up Bree."

The guys seemed to process this for a moment, then nodded solemnly.

"By the way." Doyle stepped forward with a mysterious grin. "There's someone else here to see you."

"Really? Who?" I asked, watching them exchange knowing smiles.

"Tony Etheridge," Haskell blurted out.

"Tony?" Just repeating his name made all my pain swerve into the center of my chest. *What's he doing here? Why isn't he with Bree?*

"Yeah. When you fell, he was the first one at your side," Bennett said.

"The guy came out of nowhere!" Rom added.

Oscar nodded. "He even stayed with you until the paramedics arrived."

"He did?" I asked incredulously. I could feel that sense of hope trying to return, but I shooed it away. The fact that he helped me didn't really mean anything. For all I knew, he could have been trying to cover Bree's butt.

"Anyway." Doyle leaned forward again. "We

changed our mind about him. He obviously cares about you, and he seems to be a decent person. I guess we just assumed he was a jerk since he hung out with those terrorist jocks."

I lay there, trying to sort out all that had happened to me in the last five hours. Things were way too weird, as if the world had suddenly tipped sideways. *So now the guys are big Tony fans. After urging me to forget about him?*

"So . . . should I let him in?" Doyle asked, trying to read my expression.

I hesitated. There was no way my injured brain could process it all, so I went on instinct.

"Sure," I said. "Let him in."

Doyle opened the door and mumbled something to Tony. Then, as soon as Tony stepped inside, the gang trudged out, a few of them uttering lame excuses about needing to make a phone call or wanting to find the snack machines. The door shut, and Tony remained at the back of the room, watching me.

"You sure you're up to having visitors?" he asked. "Because the nurses are kind of mad about all the people that have shown up."

"It's okay," I said.

He smiled bravely and walked over to the side of the bed. "You look great," he said, sounding somewhat nervous.

I hadn't seen myself since my final primp in front of the dressing-room mirror, but I knew by the feel of bandages and the soreness in my face that I looked anything but great. Still, I mumbled, "Thanks."

Tony suddenly collapsed down into a nearby chair and let out a huge sigh. "God, I'm glad you're okay. I'm sorry. I just don't know what to do here. I feel like I should have brought you flowers—or at least transported over the bouquet I sent you backstage."

"What?" I asked, a tingly sensation spreading through my limbs. "What are you talking about?"

He studied my baffled expression with alarm. "I had flowers sent to the dressing room for you. You don't remember?"

"No. I remember. But . . . but those were for Bree. The guy gave them to her."

It was Tony's turn to look flabbergasted. "Huh?" he mumbled. Then slowly a look of comprehension came over his face. "Oh," he breathed out, grinning slightly. "I bet I know what happened."

"What?"

"They wouldn't let me go back there, so I gave one of the club's busboys five dollars to deliver them. He didn't know English very well, so I told him to give them to the ballerina and pantomimed some moves for him. He must have thought I meant Bree's gymnastics routine." Tony shook his head and chuckled. "Guess I don't make convincing ballet moves."

"Now, wait a minute," I said, straining to raise up. "Are you saying—?" But everything went woozy, and I couldn't finish.

Tony reached over and placed his hands behind me, guiding me back down to the bed. "Hey. Take it easy," he said. After I was settled back, he let his left hand linger on my cheek. "The flowers were for you," he murmured, brushing his fingers against my skin. "I'm sorry you didn't get them."

I couldn't speak. Tears were filling my eyes, yet all my pain was melting away. I could only reach up with my good arm and take his hand in mine.

"And I'm sorry we never got that slow dance either," he said softly.

"That's okay," I whispered hoarsely. "There's still plenty of time for that."

Cameron

I tramped up the wooden porch steps and unlocked the front door to Aunt Lenore's house. It surprised me to find a light on inside and Aunt Lenore sitting in the living room. After leaving the pageant, I'd driven out to my dad's closed-up garage and thought for a long time. I figured by now everyone would be asleep.

"I'm sorry I stayed out so late," I said. "I hope you weren't waiting up."

Aunt Lenore smiled weakly. "No. The taxi just brought me back from the hospital a little while ago. Gwen Darby was hurt after she fell on the metal risers at the pageant."

"Oh no!" I exclaimed. "I'm so sorry. That thing was tough to unfold, but I thought I had it pretty sturdy."

Aunt Lenore held up a hand and shook her

head. "It was the other riser," she explained. "Apparently Blaine never checked to make sure it was locked in place. So, he and the little upstart girl who tripped her are going to be paying for Gwen's hospital bills. He'll be helping out in the club's kitchen every day after school."

I didn't know what to say. The image of Blaine Gallagher washing dishes was almost too much for the human mind to grasp.

She exhaled heavily and stood up. "Well, I'm going to try to get some sleep. I just don't know how I'll face the ladies at the club after this."

"Good night, Aunt Lenore," I said as she crossed the room to the staircase. "And . . . I'm sorry."

"Don't be, Cameron," she said. "Go to bed soon."

I stretched out on the sofa and tried to fathom everything she'd told me. But I was too tired. For the past few hours I'd done nothing but think. Not that it did me any good. The only thing I figured out was that I didn't want to think anymore—about anything. From here on out I would just fix cars. Everything else was too complicated.

Just then a light rapping sounded on the front door. Probably one of Blaine's friends coming to tell him about a late party. I opened the door, expecting to find a couple of half-drunk athletes, but instead Ashleigh stood half illuminated by the yellow porch light.

"Ash," I whispered.

"Hi," she said, grinning. "I saw the light on and thought I would knock. I wanted to give you this." She held out her hand. A folded sash made out of some red, shiny material lay in her palm. "You left before Dad made his announcement. You're the grand marshal!"

If I had been in a normal state of mind, I'd have probably been bowled over with surprise and gratitude. But after making the excruciating decision to stay in my place in the world, away from Ashleigh, I just couldn't get excited about leading a dumb parade.

"No," I said quietly. "I'm not the grand marshal."

Ash seemed confused. "Yes, you are. Dad announced it."

I shook my head. "You don't understand. I appreciate the thought, but I can't take that."

She dropped her hand and took a step toward me. "Cam, I wish you'd tell me what's going on," she said. "If there's been some sort of complication with your mom or—"

"It's not about my mom!" I practically yelled. Ash stared at me with wide, wounded eyes.

"Look," I said, toning down my voice and slouching back against the doorjamb. "I've been doing a lot of thinking, and the thing is, I just can't pretend to be somebody I'm not anymore."

"What are you talking about?" Ash asked. "What kind of pretending?"

I tugged at the collar of my blazer. "See these clothes? They're Blaine's. And the Beemer I drove around tonight was on loan from my aunt. I could never afford an expensive car, and even if I had the money for fancy clothes, I wouldn't know what to get. I hate golf, and I'm really not good at socializing. So, you see? There's no way things would work out between us."

Ashleigh's face went flat, and she slowly shook her head. "How could you . . . ?" she whispered.

"I know. I'm sorry I wasn't more honest. I just wanted a chance to go out with you. Although"—I hung my head self-consciously—"I know you probably said yes just to be nice."

In a flash Ashleigh threw the grand-marshal sash down at my feet and stomped down the steps of the porch. As soon as she hit the sidewalk, she whirled around to face me. "I can't believe you! Do you actually think I'm that shallow? Do you think I care what you wear or drive? I *liked* you, Cam. I *wanted* to go out with you."

"You . . . did?" I asked, struck by both the revelation and the past tense of her words.

"Yes!" she replied. "You're everything that matters. You're sweet and honest and humble. *That's* why I liked you. And that's why Dad chose you to be grand marshal—and why you deserve it."

I stood there, stunned, letting her words melt into me. All this time I'd been trying to figure out a way to be worthy of her and never found an answer. Then, when I thought I was doing the right thing by giving up, I blew my only chance. How could I have been so stupid?

"I . . . I'm sorry," I said softly. "I didn't know. . . ."

Ashleigh looked up at the stars and frowned. "I've got to go," she said suddenly.

"No, wait!" I called. But it was too late. Ash was already jogging toward her car, her dress swirling about her legs and strands of hair falling out of their loose knot.

And then it was over. The dream I'd had for eight years had come true and died—making me wish it had never come true at all.

Marissa

My Skechers squeaked against the freshly mopped linoleum of the hospital corridor. This place was all too familiar. The neutral-colored walls. The buzzing yellow lights. The harsh, antiseptic scents. It had been only a few months since I'd paced these halls as a human crutch for my mom while Dad lay in bypass surgery. Just being here unearthed those same fidgety, scary feelings—which I added to my present mix of fear and guilt.

I turned the corner and came to the second-floor waiting room. There was Fry. He sat forward in a square-shaped chair of orange vinyl, with his elbows on his knees and his hands covering his face. He looked so worn out, I wasn't sure if I should approach him. As I stood there, wavering, Fry slid his fingers down his forehead and rubbed his eyes, then opened his arms in a stretch.

"Fry," I called out, then quickly winced. "I mean, Brian."

He glanced over at me. At first his expression

seemed pleased and a little surprised. Then, slowly, his eyes went sad. Almost immediately he turned and stared indifferently at the wall.

Scraping up my courage, I marched right up to him and plunked down into the empty chair to his left. "How's Gwen?" I asked as if I hadn't noticed his snub.

"She's fine," he mumbled. "The doctors are releasing her tomorrow."

"That's great," I said, sighing in relief.

A tense silence followed. While Brian gazed at the waiting room's dingy blue carpet, I had a chance to inspect his wounds. My throat clamped as I noted his puffy eye and zigzag pattern of scratches. I couldn't believe it was all because of me.

"I'm so sorry, Brian!" I blurted out as my tears suddenly restarted. "I didn't mean those things I said to Will. Most of them anyway. I only said that first bad stuff because I didn't know you yet. And the other stuff I said because I didn't want my dad to find out I liked you." I took a big, shuddery breath and tried to calm down, but it only made me sound squeakier. "I know I should have stood up for you," I went on. "But I was just . . . scared."

As I rambled, I started to feel a little better. At least everything felt clearer. I lifted my head to face Brian, who was still watching me. His expression was almost tender, only his eyes still seemed wary—a look that didn't exactly pull me in, but didn't push me away either.

"I've been a total phony. I know," I murmured shakily. "Can you forgive me?"

He let out a long sigh and stared down the drab hospital corridor. "I don't know," he said.

It wasn't what I wanted to hear, but I could take it. I could understand it, even. And I was halfway grateful he didn't tell me to get lost.

We sat there without speaking. My tears had stopped, and I felt a weird sense of calm, as if I'd just ridden through a rough storm. I gazed over at Brian as he continued to contemplate the hallway. It suddenly struck me how, when I looked at him, I didn't see the tangled hair or beard stubble anymore. I just saw *him*. Brian was so much more than his appearance, the same way a painting, no matter how great, could never quite capture the real thing.

Without thinking, I reached up and touched his face, gingerly tracing his cuts and bruises. Brian's head pivoted ever so slightly toward me. I brought down my hand and kissed my fingertips, pressing them softly against his wounds. Then I did it again and again.

Each time his body inched closer toward me until finally Brian grabbed my hand in his and pulled me to him, pressing his mouth to mine.

WELCOME TO KINGSTOWN'S ANNUAL FALL FESTIVAL!

Meet the Fall Fest Beauty and Talent Queen!

Today's Events
Chicken-Flying Contest 9 A.M.
Jalapeño-Eating Contest 10 A.M.

Judging of Beard-Growing Contest 11 A.M.
Chili Cook-off 12 noon

<u>and</u> <u>at</u> 2 P.M.
Mayor Witherspoon and the Fall Fest grand marshal will
signal the commencement of the festival parade!
Grab a blanket and pick a spot!
Come wave to our newly crowned queen!

Festival carnival will follow and continue till dusk

Sixteen

Gwenyth

"**A**RE YOU SURE you don't want to go home?" Tony asked for the eighteenth time, grasping me around by my good shoulder to guide me over a curb.

"I'm fine," I said. "Really."

I was so glad when the doctors released me from the county hospital in plenty of time to make it to the parade. Tony had worked it out with Brian to pick me up, and he thought I was nuts when I asked him to take me downtown. But for some bizarre reason, I really wanted to come. It just seemed like I was part of it all now. And if you didn't count the sling on my left arm and the last traces of a headache I had, I really did feel up to it. Only Tony didn't seem to believe me.

"Okay. I'm going to ask you one last time," he said, trotting in a half circle to stand in front of me.

"Are you positive you can do this? Your brother will probably send *me* to the hospital if anything happens to you."

"We could share an ambulance," I remarked.

Tony shook his head. "Not funny."

I grinned mischievously and tucked a tuft of hair behind his ear. "You're sweet," I murmured. "But I'm going to be fine. Really."

Tony cradled my chin in his hand and kissed me lightly on the mouth—something else he'd been doing a lot of since he met me at the hospital. Not that I was complaining.

"Hey! Tony and Gwen!" someone called.

The voice eventually reached our brains, and we broke away from each other. We looked over and saw Tracy Reed standing a few yards off, waving to us. She was standing on a large, quilted blanket with Sherry Wynn, Lori Harris, and all the rest of Bree's crowd. Only Bree was nowhere in sight—and neither was Linda Loftin, who was probably on the queen's float, getting ready for the parade.

Tony and I exchanged a short, bewildered glance and headed over.

"Oh, Gwen!" Tracy crooned when we reached their blanket. "How are you?"

"I'm better, thanks."

"We were just talking about how horrible you must feel!" she went on. "First you get hurt, and then you lose the title! You must be so upset!"

I shrugged slightly. "I'm all right."

"Well, if I were you, I'd sue or something," Sherry added.

"Yeah. And we all think Bree should be suspended," Lori jumped in.

I glanced around at each of their faces. It was strange to see them so animated. Of course, normally their chatter was strictly controlled by Bree.

A realization crept over me: I really did it. I shook up the status quo and knocked Bree off her throne. Should I congratulate myself? After all, it was one of the reasons why I'd entered the pageant. For some reason, though, I didn't feel all that victorious.

Guess they'll need a new leader now, I mused. *But who will it be? Tracy? Linda? Lori?*

"Sit down, you two," Tracy said, patting an empty spot on the quilt.

"Yeah, you *have* to sit with us," Lori added. "We want to hear *everything*."

"And you can tell us what you think when Linda comes down on the float," said Sherry.

The way they were staring at me seemed somewhat familiar. Then I remembered. They used to look at Bree the same way whenever they listened to her talk. *No!* I thought, taking an instinctive step backward. *This isn't what I wanted. I don't want to be the new Bree!*

As if reading my mind, Tony put his arm around me and squeezed my good shoulder. "Thanks for asking," he said to Tracy and the rest, "but we're sitting somewhere else."

"Really?" Tracy seemed completely taken aback. "Where?"

Yeah, I thought. *Where?*

"With them," he said, pointing across the street. I turned and followed the line of his finger. There, perched under the shade of a droopy mimosa tree, sat Doyle and the rest of my gang.

I caught Tony's eye and smiled broadly, communicating unspoken gratitude.

At that moment Doyle glanced up and saw us. "Hey!" he called, cupping his hands over his mouth. "Hey, Gwen! Tony!"

"You know . . . ," Tracy whispered, her mouth curled in revulsion, "you don't have to sit with those guys anymore."

"That's right." Sherry nodded. "With Bree gone, you can sit with us again."

"I know I don't *have* to sit with them," I replied. "But I want to."

"Come on, Gwen. Let's go grab our seats before the parade starts," Tony said, gently pulling me away from them. "You all have fun, okay?"

I could practically feel the girls' openmouthed stares as we crossed Main Street. I was certain they'd spend the rest of the day, and possibly beyond, talking all about us. And for once I truly didn't care.

"Hey, Tony?" I said, reaching for his hand. "What's your favorite video game?"

He shook his head, chuckling. "I don't know. What does it matter?"

"Oh, it matters," I said as our gang loomed into view. "Believe me, it matters."

Marissa

"Hey, look at that one!" Brian cried, pointing down at a float in the shape of a giant, coiled rattlesnake. "Its tail moves and everything. How cool!"

"That's probably the animal club's," I remarked.

We sat on a grassy hill under the water tower, which gave us a fantastic view of the parade start. A dense, crooked line of floats, band members, and horseback riders packed the easternmost end of North Street. From there they would turn onto Main and continue for two miles until they reached Amherst.

Brian reached into his cooler bag and pulled out a brown bottle. "Root beer?" he asked.

"Sure."

He twisted off the cap and tossed it back in the bag. Then he handed me the bottle and slid up next to me, his shoulder touching mine.

I glanced over at him, taking in his profile. It was obvious the minute Brian met me at the door to his house that he'd worked more on his appearance today. He'd brushed his hair. It was amazing, but he looked like a different person, like a rock star.

When I saw him, my first impulse had been to tell him how great he looked, but I held back. I didn't want him to think that mattered to me. Because it didn't. It really, really didn't.

Besides, I'd transformed myself a little too. Instead of black I'd opted for a white T-shirt and blue jeans. It wasn't exactly for Brian's benefit. I just wasn't in a black mood anymore.

"There's the float the art classes made," I said, pointing to a flatbed trailer that just joined the line. On it sat a giant plywood structure of your stereotypical painter's palette and paintbrush.

"That thing?" Brian exclaimed. "Yuck! We could do better than that."

"Yeah," I agreed. "Maybe we should partner up to do one for the next parade?"

He nodded. "Maybe. If *I* get to do the sketches."

I bumped him with my shoulder.

"By the way," Brian said, his face turning serious. "How's your dad dealing with all this?"

I smiled. "He apologized to me! Do you believe it? He said he owed you an apology too. And that the next time I invited you over, he'd be sure and give it to you." I shook my head, still unable to wrap my mind around how great my dad was when he heard the whole story. "I finally told my father how worried I was about his health, how afraid I was to do anything that might upset him. We had a long talk, and he told me to stop worrying so much. And then we hugged. That's why I've been so afraid of confessing—"

Brian squeezed my hand. "You don't have to explain, Marissa. I think I understand. I'm just glad everything's all worked out."

"And," I continued, "he's finally changed his

mind about Will Benson. You know, I heard he and Lenny are going to have to pay fines and do lots of community service."

"The dude got off easy," Brian muttered through a clenched jaw.

"At least it's over," I said, trying to keep the conversation light. "Oh! I almost forgot! Chief Huxtable called and said you and I are eligible for the hundred-dollar reward since we helped catch them."

Brian's eyebrows lifted. "Really? What do you know."

"Maybe we should celebrate?" I suggested.

"We could eat out somewhere," he said, rubbing his chin.

"Or spend it on some decent art supplies," I added.

Brian shook his head. "No," he said decisively. "I know what we should do with it."

"What?"

"We should give it to Ms. Crowley so she can put it toward the new airbrush she's been wanting. After all"—he looked at me with a smug grin—"if it wasn't for her, we might have never gotten together."

"You're right," I said, smiling. It seemed unreal that I had begged Ms. Crowley not to make me work with him. Maybe she'd known what she was doing all along. Or maybe it was just fate. Either way, it did seem like I owed her. "To Ms. Crowley," I said, holding up my bottle.

"To Ms. Crowley," he echoed.

We clinked bottles and drank, turning to stare

out at the parade assembly. A second later I felt his arm drape around my back and pull me to him. As I leaned over and settled my head on his shoulder, long-forgotten emotions washed over me. For the first time in months, I was happy.

Cameron

Please don't let me be too late!

As I raced down North Street, weaving around trucks and horses and the occasional stray juggler, the red sash Aunt Lenore had pinned across me tugged at my clothing. Finally I caught sight of the head float—a flatbed draped with flags and crepe paper, with a giant three-tiered pyramid for the riders to stand on. Ashleigh was already standing on top of it. In fact, it was her long, gold hair waving in the light breeze that had first grabbed my attention. Mr. Witherspoon stood below, chatting with a group of kids on bicycles.

"Ashleigh! Mayor Witherspoon!" I called as I approached the float.

Ashleigh immediately whirled around. "You came," she said, sounding surprised. Then a cloud crossed her features, and she turned away again, frowning in the direction of a nearby clown.

"I'm so sorry I'm late," I gasped as I reached the truck. "I'd promised Aunt Lenore I'd help her with the queen's float."

Mayor Witherspoon clapped me hard on the

back. "No problem. These things never start on time anyway."

Ashleigh continued to stare into the distance. I wished I had arrived earlier. I had so much to say to her, but there was no way we could really talk with her dad there.

"Sorry you missed the big announcement last night," the mayor went on. "But I see you got your sash."

"Yes, sir. And I hope this is good enough for the grand marshal to wear," I said, gesturing at my blue jeans and Kingstown High T-shirt. "I don't want to put on another suit for a long time."

Mayor Witherspoon burst out laughing. "Don't worry about that," he said. "In fact, I'll let you in on a piece of classified information." He quickly glanced to either side of him and leaned closer, lowering his voice to a mere normal tone. "When I have to ride in the car at the head of the Fourth of July parade each year, it's always so dad-burned hot. So I make sure I wear a nice-pressed shirt, jacket, tie, *and* my most comfortable pair of shorts. After all, no one can see them when I sit in the car!"

I laughed, wondering how Aunt Lenore would react to his little secret. The more I got to know Mayor Witherspoon, the more I liked him.

The mayor's chuckles waned, and he squinted down at his watch. "I'm going to go ask Chief Huxtable when we're starting. Stay here and guard the float."

I watched as he lumbered up to a nearby squad

car and poked his head through the passenger-side window. Now was my chance. Quickly I scrambled onto the float and approached Ashleigh.

"Hey, Ash," I murmured, "could I speak with you for a second?"

She turned around and raised her eyebrows impatiently.

Fiddling with the frayed end of my sash, I forced myself to speak. "I'm sorry for the way I acted, and I wouldn't blame you if you never spoke to me again. But I just wanted to say that I was wrong. I should have known you'd never judge people that way."

Her expression remained unchanged.

"I just went a little crazy, I guess," I continued. "Anyway, I'm sorry. And I'm sorry for cutting out on you at the pageant. And I'm sorry I was all put out when you came to see me. And I'm sorry I took eight years to ask you out. And I'm sorry—"

"Stop," she said suddenly.

I looked at her, confused.

Ashleigh tilted her head at me, a smile slowly making its way across her face. "It's okay," she said, sighing. "You're forgiven."

"I am?"

"Yes," she said, laughing lightly. "You're way too sweet for me to stay mad at you, Cameron."

I couldn't believe it. My heart seemed to sputter back to life. I felt like I could launch myself into the air and soar like a plane.

Just then the float rocked as Mayor Witherspoon climbed on board.

"Grab ahold of something," he said, stationing himself at the front of the float. "We're about to start."

I reached out and grabbed Ashleigh's hand. We smiled quietly at each other as the float lurched forward.

"Yeehaw!" Mayor Witherspoon shouted, waving to the crowd. "Finally! We waited long enough, don't you think? Time to get this show on the road!"

"Yep," I said, squeezing Ashleigh's hand. "It's about time."

Is Your Crush Boyfriend Material?

If only your crush was your boyfriend, right? You'd be so happy! Or would you . . . ? Take our quiz and find out if he's a prince charming . . . a prince in training . . . or a prince uncharming:

1. When you see your crush, he:
a. Ignores you
b. Smiles but says nothing
c. Stops to have a convo in the halls

2. When he's around his friends, he:
a. Acts a little differently
b. Includes you in the convo
c. Friends? What friends?

3. You ask him about his last girlfriend, and he says:

a. Eww! Who wants to talk about that loser?
b. We broke up, but we're still friends
c. Can we change the subject?

4. It's the night of the school dance, but the basketball play-offs are on TV, so he asks:
a. Can we compromise by watching the game a little and then go to the dance?
b. Do we have to go to the dance?
c. What color corsage would you like?

5. You and your crush are playing word association. You say "couple," and he says:
a. What?
b. Yes
c. Yuck

6. During lunch he notices the new guy is sitting alone. He:
   a. Invites the guy to join his buds at their regular table
   b. Taunts him like some other guys are doing
   c. Introduces himself and welcomes him to the school

7. There's a substitute teacher in class today. Your crush:
   a. Gets up on the desk and screams, *"Party!"*
   b. Is studying for the test next period in the back of the room
   c. Acts as if the regular teacher were present

8. Your bff calls his house to talk to you, and he:
   a. Gets annoyed—the two of you had been making out
   b. Hands you the phone and tells you not to stay on long
   c. Chats a bit, then leaves the room to give you privacy

9. His best friend just got dumped by his girlfriend. Your crush's advice is:
   a. She wasn't that pretty anyway
   b. To tell her how he feels
   c. "Let's go shoot some hoops and talk about it."

10. You want to meet his parents, and his reply is:
   a. Sure, how about dinner tomorrow?
   b. Um, er, well, um . . .
   c. Honestly, I'm not ready for that yet

1.	a 1	b 2	c 3
2.	a 2	b 3	c 1
3.	a 2	b 3	c 1
4.	a 2	b 1	c 3
5.	a 2	b 3	c 1
6.	a 3	b 1	c 2
7.	a 1	b 2	c 3
8.	a 1	b 2	c 3
9.	a 1	b 2	c 3
10.	a 3	b 1	c 2

If he scored from 10 to 17:

Prince *Uncharming*

Uh-oh! He might be cute, but that doesn't mean he's mature enough—or deserving enough—for a great girl like you. This guy's more interested in acting like a jerk so that he'll seem like a "cool" guy to his friends. But it reality, he's anything but cool. And he won't make you a very good boyfriend at all. Maybe in a couple of years . . .

If he scored from 18 to 24:

Prince in Training

This guy's almost ready to be a great boyfriend but needs a little training in that department. That just means you might have to risk getting angry or upset when he does something that seems insensitive. Otherwise he won't change. If you can call him on what bugs you and praise him for what makes you feel all warm and fuzzy inside, you just might help turn him into the best boyfriend in the world.

If he scored from 25 to 30:

Prince!
This guy is ready for a relationship, ready to treat his girlfriend like gold, ready to balance everything in his life: school, his friends, his hobbies, and his girlfriend. Not only does he make your knees weak, but he's a *nice* guy. And that's the best thing any girl can say about her boyfriend. That's truly what makes a guy a prince.

Do you ever wonder about falling in love? About members of the opposite sex? Do you need a little friendly advice but have no one to turn to? Well, that's where we come in . . . Jenny and Jake. Send us those questions you're dying to ask, and we'll give you the straight scoop on life and love.

DEAR JAKE

Q: *Do guys like it when girls wear makeup?*
JT, Branson, MO

A: Hmmm . . . I definitely don't have a yes or no answer. I like it when girls wear makeup, and I like it when they don't. I tend to be attracted to girls who wear very little makeup, but then again, when my last "granola" girlfriend wore makeup, I thought she looked great. It all depends, I guess. I don't think any guy would like it if a girl wore makeup to play softball or go for a hike in the woods. But for a date or a dance, why not? It's really up to the girl and depends on what she likes. That tends to be just fine with us guys.

DEAR JENNY

Q: *I've had five boyfriends this year, and some of the girls at school are beginning to talk about me. It's not like I'm doing anything worth talking about. All I've done with my boyfriends is make out. But if people are talking about me, does that mean I have a bad reputation?*

DL, Monticello, NY

A: It feels awful to be the subject of gossip. But take heart: They might not be talking about you in a mean way; they might be talking about you because they're simply interested or curious. Perhaps they're wondering what you've got that they don't (like a great personality!).

Do you have any questions about love?
Although we can't respond individually to your letters,
you just might find your questions answered in our column.

Write to:
Jenny Burgess or Jake Korman
c/o 17th Street Productions,
an Alloy Online, Inc. company.
33 West 17th Street
New York, NY 10011

Don't miss any of the books in 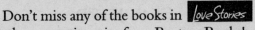 —the romantic series from Bantam Books!

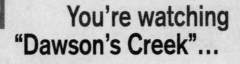

You'll always remember your first love.